BLUE

L.E. DELANO

Blue

gaze publishing

ISBN
978-1-7364731-0-8 (print)
978-1-7364731-1-5 (eBook)

*This book is dedicated to the Swoon Squad—
the best, most supportive group of authors I've ever
had the privilege of sharing an imprint with. I never
would have survived publishing without you.*

SOMETIME AROUND 350 BC, King Philip II of Macedon decided to invade Greece, and was mostly successful until he set his sights on the kingdom of Sparta. Philip decided to give the Spartans a chance to avoid bloodshed and lay down their arms before he conquered them, so he sent out a message that read: "You are advised to submit without further delay, for if I bring my army into your land I will destroy your farms, slay your people, and raze your city."

The Spartans replied with only one word.

"If."

And based on the power and implied message of that one word (and the Spartans' well-known reputations), Philip decided the Spartans weren't worth the risk, and he left them alone.

"If" is a word with the power to alter destiny. So many lives have been decided by two little letters.

If only she'd taken that job instead of this one. If we just hadn't decided to go out that day. If he'd only told her he loved her. If the baby had lived.

If only my mother hadn't named me Blue.

She thought it was pretty, maybe even a little mystical. Instead, it turned out to be a self-fulfilling prophecy. One little turn of events has completely demolished my life. One split second mistake has completely altered the trajectory of my world, and sent it tilting on its axis. I was born Blue and I'll stay blue as I drown in it all. It's so goddamn unfair.

I draw back my fist and punch the side of the slide.

"Ow! Dammit!"

I cup my hand inside the other one, blowing on them both. They were stinging bad enough before I decided to punch a hard piece of frozen plastic. The backs of my knuckles look raw, but my whole hand is bright red so it's kind of hard to tell how much damage has been done.

I trace the line on the slide wall with my finger in disbelief. It's definitely a crack. I cracked the slide when I punched it.

"I cracked it? Are you kidding me?" I say, shaking my hand out. "Un-be-freaking-lievable."

"Not really. It's simple physics."

I turn with a start and the movement jolts me free, sending me hurtling down the slide and right into the legs of the guy standing at the bottom. He jumps back, but not before I nail him in the knee with my boot.

"Oof!"

"Sorry!" I look up from my seat on the bottom of the slide, and he rubs his knee. "What the hell are you doing?" I demand. "Why are you spying on me?"

"I wasn't spying. I was here first." He smiles at me, even though I tagged his knee pretty hard. "And I came over because you looked like you hurt yourself."

I flex my fingers and look back up at the top of the slide. "Hurts like a bitch."

"You okay?"

"Yeah. What do you mean 'you were here first?'" I glare at him. He's still smiling at me, though.

He gestures toward the other side of the playground. "I was just sitting under the big plastic frog canopy, minding my own business. Here, you dropped this."

He brushes the snow off my phone and holds it out. We both look down as it vibrates in his hand and three new notifications light up the screen.

> OMG Did you hear about Maya
>
> Maya's back tomorrow
>
> Heads up - Maya's
> coming back

"Thanks," I mumble, yanking it away.

I shove the phone down in my pocket and try not to look like I want to throw up when I do. I really do. Why is he here? I didn't come to the playground in the middle of winter so I could socialize. I wanted to be alone in my misery.

He tilts his head to the slide. "Better get a move on before they arrest you for vandalism."

"Right." I actually have gloves in my pocket that I wasn't wearing because I stupidly can't stop checking my phone. I pull the right one over my sore hand. "You live around here?"

"You think I drive all over town in the freezing cold just to hang out at empty playgrounds? I live on Willow Court. On the cul-de-sac."

"I don't know what you do. I don't know you." I'm aware I'm being bitchy. And he's still smiling.

"That's because I'm new," he says. He sticks his hand out at me, like we're becoming best friends or something.

"Devon Guthrie. Moved here from Florida in December. I think we might be going to the same school."

"I can't shake your hand."

He gives me a sympathetic look. "You're sure it's not broken?"

I shrug. "And I don't go to Upper Merion," I say. "I go to a charter school—"

"Audubon Academy," he completes for me. "I think I saw you before Christmas break. We stopped by to get the paperwork. That's why I walked over to you—I thought I recognized you. Are you a senior?"

"Junior."

"Me, too.

"Oh. Well, it's a good school," I say awkwardly, cramming my gloved hands in my pocket. "I have to go."

"Not without telling me a name, I hope. It'd be nice to scream it in the halls tomorrow instead of 'Hey you.'"

He smiles again, and his teeth look really white in the darkness of the winter night. He pulls his beanie down tighter over a mop of unruly blonde hair.

"Blue." I say, as he looks at me blankly. "My name is Blue."

"First or last?"

"It's my first name." I wave off his confused look. "My mom was in her crystals and aromatherapy stage back then. The last name is Mancini."

"Blue." He repeats. "I like it." He points off to the parking lot by the playground, to an old-model powder-blue Volkswagen Bug. "I can give you a ride. I would imagine your butt is frozen into a semi-circle shape after forty minutes of laying on a slide in single-digit temps."

"Wait—you were watching me that whole time?"

"No. I was doing some thinking of my own. But I did notice when you showed up because you almost walked off the top of the platform up there looking at your phone. Whatever you saw must have you pretty upset."

I close my eyes, mortified. Did he see me crying? Cursing? Talking to myself? I'm not about to get into the whole shitfest that is my life with a guy who hangs out at playgrounds.

"Sorry." He raises his hands, palms out. "I don't need to know your business."

"It's just—" I don't want him to know my business. But if he's going to Audubon, he'll hear it all tomorrow morning. "I've kind of got a life situation going on. Sorry if I'm not at my friendliest."

"Life." He lets out a sigh. "Sucks sometimes. Still better than the alternative."

"Yeah, I guess."

For a moment, we just stand there in the quiet, with the snow falling down, looking at the ground and lost in our own thoughts. Finally, he speaks.

"So . . . you want that ride?"

"I'll walk. Thanks anyway."

He nods, readjusts his hat, and starts walking toward his car. "Sorry if I ruined your alone time," he calls back over his shoulder. "I wasn't creeping on you."

"It's okay," I call back. "I'll see you tomorrow."

"See you."

I stuff my hands in my pockets and start walking, out the gate of the playground and onto the sidewalk. The phone vibrates again and I pull it out to look at the newest text.

Maya's coming back tomorrow

What are u gonna do

What am I gonna do? How about call out sick until graduation? Hide under a desk? I want to laugh but I also want to throw my phone as hard as I can. And some weird part of me wants to get in Devon's car and tell him to drive until we're a hundred miles from here.

I look over my shoulder to make sure he's not following me, and he's not. He's just standing there by his car, arms folded, looking at me and yup—still smiling.

I don't smile back. I walk home alone in the cold, knowing I have to face tomorrow. Maybe I'll get lucky and everyone will fixate on the new guy.

A girl can hope, can't she?

I'M JUST GOING to ignore her.

What if she won't ignore me? What if she screams at me—or worse, cries? What if she tries to hit me or something? If she gets up in my face . . .

Who am I kidding? Like I'm going to say anything. Like I *can* say anything without looking like an asshole for saying it. Besides, she doesn't want to be in the same hemisphere with me. Why would she want to talk to me? She probably won't even talk to me.

But everyone else will. They'll all be lined up, wanting to hear anything we have to say about each other.

My stomach tightens so hard I feel like I'm going to puke. I glance at my phone again, and the texts from last night are still there.

> Maya's back at school

> my mom saw her mom at Target

> Maya is back

did u see her pic on IG

Did you hear about Maya

I shove the phone back down in the pocket of my coat and blow on my fingers to get them warm. I should have remembered my gloves but the whole morning is a blur and now I'm sitting in my car in the cold and I can't bring myself to turn the key in the ignition.

The phone comes out again. I have got to get a grip on myself. I know better, but I open up Instagram and find her picture. She looks good. Well, better than the last time I saw her, which wasn't a great time for her. Or me.

Last night, I stayed up trying not to obsess about this and nursing a throbbing hand—which makes me tired this morning and wishing more than anything I could go back to bed and forget the rest of this semester. I'm going to be late for school if I don't get it together. The phone drops from my hand when a fist slams repeatedly into my window, scaring the hell out of me.

"Jules!" I shriek. "What the—"

"Got tired of waiting," she says, opening the door and sliding into the passenger seat. "You better get moving or we've got another unexcused tardy."

I suppose it's a good thing she lives four houses down, but right now I wish she lived in a neighboring town and took the bus.

"Let's go." I stuff my phone down into my coat pocket, trying to ignore the way it's vibrating again. Jules's eyes drop down, having heard it.

"So is everybody all up in your business?"

"Oh God," I moan. "All day yesterday and still going this morning. This is such a non-event. It really is."

"Did you see the pic she posted?"

"Yeah, but I don't think that was meant for me."

Jules raises her brows. "You don't?"

"Nah," I say with what I hope is a careless shrug.

"Back at Audubon and nobody's gonna get me down," Jules reads aloud while looking at her phone. Obviously, she had the picture open. Maya, in her bedroom, wearing a blue hoodie and smiling, both thumbs up. Her hair is longer now and she looks really pretty.

"I think she means more like, the world in general isn't going to get her down," I tell her.

"I guess," Jules agrees, only she doesn't sound like she agrees even a little bit. "Lauren says Maya's got Poly Sci third block with Jones."

"Well then," I force a smile as I start the car. "I guess we'll find out if my theory is right."

"She better not think she can start something."

"Jules." I give her a look. "Drop it, okay? I mean, she and I barely know each other."

"I don't think that's true anymore."

"No, it's still true." I reverse out of the driveway so fast, Jules rocks sideways in her seat.

"Whoa! Don't go psycho on me! I'm just sayin'!"

"And I'm just saying; drop it. I've got enough of a feeding frenzy going on around me without you hopping on the boat, too."

"You really don't think that pic was meant for you?"

I turn to glare at her. "You honestly think I'm trying to keep Maya down? Like I don't want her to succeed? In spite of —in spite of everything?"

Jules holds up her hands, finally realizing, I guess, that my nerves are a jangling, dangling mess.

"I'm not busting on you. I'm on your side, remember?"

"There aren't any sides here," I remind her with a sigh. "Not for her, or for me. Neither one of us had a thing to do with it."

"Yeah, but dude—your brother killed her *Dad*."

I put the car in gear and drive.

LOVE IS A VERB. My mom says that. I think she and Dad heard it in a marriage counseling session once. Love is a verb. An active choice.

Except when it's not. Like when you're supposed to love somebody, maybe even did love somebody—and probably still love somebody, only you just don't feel it right now. That doesn't mean you won't feel like loving them again someday, eventually. Or maybe even forever. You're just sort-of overwhelmed right now. You're too upset or too pissed or too busy dealing with all the stuff flying at you that was kicked up by their drama.

And maybe it's drama you had no part in creating, but got sucked into anyway.

So I think you've got a right to move that word—love—from verb to noun status if it's not an action you can comfortably take right now. It's just a thing in the background, like a table or a lamp. You know it's there, and it's not going anywhere, but until you need to use it, it's not getting put into motion.

So yeah, I love my brother. But somebody died and we're not exactly on speaking terms right now.

My brother isn't some gun-waving lunatic. He didn't rob Maya's dad and shoot him down in cold blood, or anything. Jack graduated with honors and was co-captain of the hockey team. He had a big scholarship to Northeastern University in Boston and a 4.2 weighted GPA. Then he miscalculated his speed on a curve, and his blood test showed alcohol just under the legal limit. One little mistake added to another little mistake, a man's life ended, and Maya doesn't have a dad anymore.

Maya's dad may have been texting while he drove, but that couldn't be conclusively proven since the text stopped mid-sentence and was never sent—therefore no time stamp. My brother's skid marks showed him over-correcting into the opposite lane and that could have sent the other car off the steep embankment. The car flipped multiple times, and Maya's father suffered a traumatic brain injury upon impact, level three on the Glasgow Coma Scale.

I remember that part from the trial, because the prosecutor must have brought it up a half-dozen times. There were diagrams of the accident scene, diagrams of the head injury—and worse, pictures. There were charts and doctor's reports and EMT reports and police reports. And in the end, it didn't mean much because my parents have a really, really, good lawyer and he knew what he was doing. When we broke for lunch, Maya's mother agreed to a plea bargain, reducing Jack's sentence and the case was settled.

Jack lost his license for ninety days for underage drinking and is currently serving a six-month sentence in a special boot camp program. He also has to complete a couple of alcohol awareness courses while he's there, and when all that's done, his scholarship will still be waiting and he goes on with his life.

Me? I get to go to school with the fallout from this mess. I get to face Maya in the halls and wonder if she's going to scream at me the way she screamed at Jack outside the courtroom that day. I get to worry that her mom will pick her up from school and I'll see her, too. I get to deal with everyone running their mouths to my face and behind my back.

Jack, you're an asshole.

So Maya's back to school at Audubon Academy after nearly a year of being home schooled. Why? We've only got a semester before the end of the year—she couldn't have let it ride? I want to know what changed her mind but like hell I'm going to ask her.

It's completely unreasonable to think she's doing it to get at me, but it feels that way. And I know, I know . . . I'm a horribly selfish person for making it all about me. After all, I'm not the girl who tragically lost her father.

I'm just the sister of the guy that killed him, or so my best friend tells me. Honestly, Jules is lousy at being a sympathetic friend sometimes. I don't need her to kick anyone's ass. I just need her and everyone to leave it all alone. For Maya's sake, and for mine.

Jules wants to stop by Dunkin Donuts drive-thru on the way in. Might as well, we're already late. We're not going to be any less tardy with five more minutes on the clock. And that also pretty much guarantees nobody will be in the halls to talk about me—or scream in my face—since the bell will have already rung.

We sign in at the office under the stern eye of Mrs. Johnson, who is stapling a stack of papers together.

"Here you are," she says, offering the stack to someone over my shoulder. She glances down at me. "Blue, don't you have Mrs. Linza for this block?"

I look up from the sign-in sheet. "Uh-huh, AP Literature."

"Would you mind escorting Devon? He's new at Audubon this semester."

I hear him chuckle as I turn around. Guess I missed him sitting there since we were in such a rush.

"Yeah," I mutter. "Okay."

Like I need this. One more excuse for people to stare at me when I walk in with the new guy. Jules gives me a look over her shoulder as she starts off to her first block, and I gesture towards the 300 Hall as Devon holds the door for me.

"Were you late just for me?" he asks, giving me a flirty smile as he falls into step beside me. I stop in the middle of the hall.

"Look, Devon—I'm kind of not looking for a boyfriend right now. I have this—thing—with this one guy and it's whatever, but I just don't want you wasting your time."

"Meeting someone new is never a waste of time," he says. "And if you have a *thing* that's *whatever*, I can respect that. Sorry if it feels like I'm stalking you."

His smile doesn't fade a bit as he talks, and I can't tell if he's making fun of me or not.

"No, it's fine. Sorry. I'm just having a day."

"The day just started."

"Tell me about it." I roll my eyes, and we keep walking. "Linza's class is up here on the left, room 301. My brother had her and he says she's cool."

"What grade is your brother?" Devon asks, and my hand clenches tighter around the strap of my backpack.

"He's out." I grab the door handle and yank it open, a little too hard since it would have bounced off the wall if Devon hadn't grabbed it. He gives me a curious look and then he dutifully hands Mrs. Linza his paperwork. After she introduces him, he takes a seat two away from me in the same row.

I manage to do a credible job of pretending to pay attention, even though Maya's best friend Haylee is staring daggers at me—they're like pinpricks on the back of my neck. She's probably texting about me right now, too. The temptation is strong to break out my phone and see if anything's been posted anywhere, but I'm second row from the front so I don't dare. Probably better, anyway. I keep telling people to leave it alone but I'm finding it hard to take my own advice.

I suck it up, answer a few questions and try to look attentive, all while glancing around every so often in what I hope is a subtle way to make sure they're not all watching me to see if I'm worried about them watching me. Finally, Mrs. Linza hands out our first reading assignment: *Fahrenheit 451*.

Astronomy is next, and it's only around the corner in the 200 Hall. People file out, and I try to tell myself they're not looking back at me even though Haylee already gave me a side-eye as she moved past and everyone else watched her do it, too.

A finger taps my shoulder.

"Hey—you okay?" Devon says it quietly, but I see Mrs. Linza's sympathetic look and it makes me even saltier about the whole situation. I barely glance at him as I shrug into my backpack.

"I'm fine."

He nods, but the smile seems more cautious now. "Well, see ya around," he says, and he's out the door, too.

"See ya," I mumble.

One block down, one to go, and then lunch.

Lunch at the same time as Maya, since we both have the same Poly Sci class, and your third block determines your lunch.

Good. We'll get it over with before we're stuck in a classroom together. She'll probably be too busy at lunch catching up with everyone, anyway. I'm making more out of this than I need to.

Yes, I definitely am. I am going to get through this day. And then I am going to inhale a bag of Cheetos while watching bad reality shows on Netflix with a dog on my lap and a charcoal mask on my face and tomorrow will be easier. Today is easier already, with one block down.

Do I sound like a plucky optimist? Of course, I don't. I'm a realist, and time is a finite thing. There's only so much of it to devote to this stuff. People get over things. People move on.

I hope.

SEEING MAYA WAS surprisingly uneventful. We passed each other in the hallway just after second block. Of course, her posse was whispering in her ear and giving me death glares as they all moved by, and my girls–Jules, Lauren, and Other Julia were behind me doing the same stuff. It kind of makes me wonder if Maya is as tired of it all as I am.

Anyway, Maya was no big deal. She didn't even look mad. She just looked straight through me, and if that's how she wants to play it, that works for me. Honestly, it's pretty damn gracious of her and I'm very grateful. She's obviously trying to move past all this. And I want that for her. I'm not loving the idea of being a walking reminder of what she's lost. I imagine it's like someone spraying salt on the gaping wound in her chest every time she sees me.

Looking at her today made me feel like I was carrying Jack's full one hundred and sixty-five pounds on my shoulders, and that just lightened considerably.

I walk into the cafeteria on rubbery legs, relief flooding my body. It's going to be okay.

Grabbing my lunch, I remember there's nobody to eat with. Jules and my other friends have second lunch. I'm in first lunch, and the only one I know well enough to eat with is Austin.

I wasn't kidding when I said he and I were *whatever*. That pretty much defines it. We dated in tenth grade and we were intense at first—expected when he's the guy who took my v-card but then he ghosted me. That sucked a *lot*, but I got over it and dated a few other people until he suddenly remembered me at the end of last semester. He said things 'slipped away' with him concentrating on football and college. He's a senior and hoping for a scholarship so he's got a lot going on. We started hanging again, mostly because I was lonely and he didn't want the hassle of finding somebody new. That's how it feels most of the time, anyway.

I mean, if you really like someone, you open your mouth and explain that shit instead of ghosting them and expecting to just pick up where you left off. Which is what we're kind of doing, so, yeah, I don't take my own advice. He was really busy over Christmas break so we pretty much only texted. But it's fine because we can catch up in person right now, if I even want to. He's got to make the first move, though. I'm not panting after him.

I throw my coat over a chair, slide down into it, and pull out my phone. My eyes casually scan the cafeteria, looking for Austin's favorite red hoodie. I stare down at my phone again and frown at Haylee's latest pic—her and Maya by the lockers with a caption about having fun in spite of *"the stank in the halls."* Nice.

I look up and spot Devon over at the cashier. We make eye contact, but I don't really acknowledge him and look back down at my phone. This time, I check Maya's pics, and suck in an audible breath before I cover it and force a calm look on my face.

"💙 *Lunch* 💙 " she wrote, right under a pic that had to have been taken moments ago here in the cafeteria, judging by the bank of windows to the side and the poster for the spring musical on the wall behind her. And sitting next to her, in a new blue hoodie he must've gotten for Christmas, wearing a smile as Maya's lips intersect his cheek—is Austin.

What???

How???

He doesn't even know Maya! Does he?

Well, obviously he does.

I stuff the phone in my pocket, and consider leaving, but like hell I'm going to let them know I'm bothered. Not that I am. I mean, Austin and I aren't really together. Definitely not now. I turn my head toward the cashier.

"Devon!" I call out with a wave.

His perpetual grin widens as he walks over, drops his tray on the table and slides into the chair across from me.

"Changed your mind, huh? I can sit with you now?"

"I thought you might have questions, since it's your first day," I make my lips curve into a smile as my hand curls into a fist under the table.

"And you thought your *whatever* boyfriend should see you sitting with the new guy," he says matter-of-factly. He has an orange on his tray, and he peels it as he talks. I start to protest but he chuckles and keeps peeling. "No, it's okay. Glad to be of service. Is that him in the pic with the girl you're supposed to fight?"

"Jesus." I say under my breath. "News travels fast around here."

"Turns out I have your friend for second block. Julia."

"Which one?"

"Huh?"

"Which Julia?" I ask absently, trying to look casual as my eyes slide again toward the corner where Maya and Austin are sitting.

"How many Julia's do you hang with?" He asks.

"There's Jules—that's Julia Franklin. And then there's Julia Rosenberg. We call her Other Julia because Jules is really Julia, too and both nicknames sort-of evolved over time."

I try to look like I'm not staring as I talk. Austin is saying something and Maya is laughing like he's God's gift to comedy.

"The Julia in the office this morning," Devon supplies. "She sits right next to me in Graphic Design. Thanks to her, I think I'm up to speed on everything with you now."

My eyes swing back to him and narrow. "Is that so?"

"Don't be pissed at your friend. I just wanted to know what book you had inside you."

"Huh?"

"*Fahrenheit 451*," he says with an off-handed wave. "I guess you haven't read it yet."

"We just got it today," I remind him.

"Well, it's a classic. Ray Bradbury is a master. It's set in a futuristic society where books are outlawed and burned if they're found. There's this underground movement to preserve them, so each person memorizes their favorite book. It becomes their story to tell. And I was wondering about your story, is all."

"No one wants a book about me," I say glumly. But I definitely could write one right now. Except I'm not the hero, or the villain. Who writes a book about an innocent bystander? I'm the girl at the intersection, who gets splashed by the mud puddle as the cars go by. Right now, Maya is flinging more mud my way. And Jules is apparently holding a garden hose and making sure there's mud for everybody. Worst of all, I have to stand here and let it swamp me. It's not like I can call her out without looking like a colossal bitch, considering the circumstances.

"Jules had no right to talk about me," I grumble.

"She was doing you a favor," Devon says. I raise my brows silently, but he presses on. "C'mon, you have to know everyone is talking about you today. I was bound to hear it all. Wouldn't you rather I hear your story from someone who really knows you?"

"I'd rather everybody just shut the hell up." I look down at my cold slice of pizza and start picking cheese from the edge of it. "So, what did Jules tell you?"

"That your brother was drunk and coming home from a party and crashed into Maya's dad—who was texting. Maya's dad died, your brother got off easy, and now Maya blames you for it all."

"Jack wasn't legally drunk," I defend, inwardly fuming at Julia. "The officer at the scene had a broken breathalyzer, so he gave Jack a field sobriety test. He only failed it because he has ADHD and his meds can affect his balance. They blood tested him at the hospital later and he was below the legal limit."

That was the defense my parent's ten-thousand-dollar retainer-so-far of a lawyer planned to give to the judge. An argument could be made that Jack fell below the legal limit because it took nearly ninety minutes for him to get to the hospital due to his lack of life-threatening injuries, very backed-up traffic and the fact that their crash site was right on the line between two ambulance companies, so both came out and had to figure out who was going where. By the time his blood was drawn at the hospital, Jack was just barely under the limit.

But that argument was never made, because of the plea agreement. And of course, Jack was a bright young man with no previous record, a hockey scholarship and a good future ahead of him who, while underage, was technically not drunk enough to be classified as legally drunk.

All of that means less than nothing to Maya—and I guess to Jules and the rest of the school, too. And even though the gossip might be tinged with truth, Jack is still my brother. And Maya's Dad was probably texting while driving. The circumstances did show reasonable doubt as to who was ultimately at fault in that courtroom, but not so much in the court of public opinion, where I'm guilty by association if I dare try to defend my brother.

"Sorry," Devon says, lifting his hands in apology.

"People love to write their own stories," I ever-so-slightly tilt my head in Maya's direction. "Even when they're not entirely supported by the facts."

"That's why I'm talking to you," Devon says. "You don't have to tell me all of it. I'm only interested in the parts that affect you."

"It all affects me. I swear to God, my mom named me Blue so I would be perpetually miserable."

"Nope." Devon takes a drink of his lemonade. "Blue is beautiful. Like the sky. Like the wide-open sky."

I give him a sour look for trying to make light of all this. "Whatever," I say.

"So, I'm a *whatever* now? Don't you already have one of those?" He pops the last segment of orange in his mouth.

I glance at Austin, who—dammit—is looking at me now. "Apparently not." I say as I wad up my napkin and drop it on my pizza. "It's fine. He was a waste of time, anyway. You done?"

He shakes his head with a mouthful of orange.

I stand up, shoving my chair back. "I need to get something from my car."

He tries valiantly to chew and say something, but I'm gone before he can clear his mouth. I want to look to the right to see if Maya or Austin notice me leaving, but I manage to keep my eyes on the door. Then I'm in the hallway and through the doors, running until I'm out in the bitter, gray January cold without my coat. And of course, my car keys are in my coat pocket, back in the cafeteria.

I lean back against the cold brick wall, and refuse to let myself cry. I need a minute. Just one undisturbed minute with no one giving me scathing or sympathetic looks, with no one whispering or posting pictures or cuddling up to the guy I thought I liked or telling other people what they think is my life story. Just one freaking minute so I can breathe.

I don't even get that. Just as the traitorous tears spill over, the door next to me opens and Devon rushes out. He stops, looks around, and then jumps when he finally sees me.

"Whoa!" He exclaims. "Sorry—did I hit you with the door?"

"I'm fine." I rub at my cheeks with the back of my frozen hands. "I just need this day to be over with."

His eyes soften, and yet another look of sympathy makes me clench my teeth.

"It'll be over with soon enough," he says. "You're halfway there. Here—you forgot your stuff." He sets my backpack on the ground and holds my coat out to me. With a grateful nod, I slide my arms into it, zipping it up tight.

"You should go back inside."

"You, too. Don't want your book to end with you becoming a Popsicle."

"My book ends when my miserable life ends," I say darkly. "After several more decades of torture."

"Don't say that!" He blurts out. "Your life isn't miserable. It just feels that way right now. It's all about perspective. What you do to move forward."

I choke on a sarcastic laugh. "No one is going to let me move forward."

"Sure they will. They'll get bored eventually. You just keep busy until they do. Focus on the good things."

Great. Just what I need—sunshine and unicorns. I know he's trying to help but I am *not* in the mood.

"Thanks," I say, but I don't mean it and he knows it. I grab my backpack, pull the door open and he falls into step beside me as we walk down the hall.

"Cheer up." He bumps my shoulder with his. "You've done a good deed today by helping me. That's a positive."

"I walked you to your English class," I remind him. "That's not exactly Nobel prize material."

"I'm not talking about that," he goes on. "You made my first day at a new school a complete non-event. Nobody's even noticed me with all the drama swirling around you."

I'm not grateful to be reminded of that. "Why—is your inner book not interesting enough?"

Something flashes for a moment in his eyes. "No one gets to read my book," he says, and his smile fades slightly. "Not until I kill the villain."

He saunters off, hands in his pockets.

"WE'RE GOING TO SEE Jack on Sunday," Mom says as she nudges the bowl of roasted kale towards me. My hand stops it before it can get too near. I hate kale. And I hate when Mom and I eat dinner by ourselves because that means her focus is entirely on me.

I take the smallest possible portion of chicken I can get away with, and carve it up on my plate. The sooner it goes down, the sooner I'm back in my room.

"Well?" Mom asks.

I look up at her with a mouthful of chicken. "Well what?'

"I said we're going to see Jack," she repeats, "and I'd like us to go as a family."

"Like the way we eat dinner as a family?" My chin points to the empty chair at the head of the dining room table. "Why do we even bother? We should just get take-out and sit on the couch when Dad works late."

"You know he can't help it," Mom says sharply. She pushes the bowl of kale toward me again. "Put some green on your plate. Please."

I toy with the idea of taking some just to get her off my back, then feeding it to the dog when she's not looking, but even Mojo won't eat kale.

"I'm good," I tell her.

She makes a face. "Would you rather have one of the super spirulina shakes? They taste just like mango water ice."

"Mango water ice isn't chalky. Or green," I remind her. Nice try with making it sound like something enjoyable, but I know better. Mom has been selling diet shakes—oh, excuse me—*lifestyle* shakes for a couple of months now. It's her latest woman-empowering venture into Boss Babe entrepreneurship, and from what I can tell, it's all the same sales pitch, with a slightly different product.

We have shelves full of powdered protein shake mix in the garage, right next to the boxes of revolutionary skin care products—three different brands, maybe more. It's hard to keep track because she cycles through a new multi-level marketing company about every eight or nine months, and sometimes there's overlap. Along with shakes and anti-wrinkle cream are the herbal supplements, spice dips and kitchen gadgets, tote bags and lunchboxes with bright patterns, boxes of clunky, overpriced silver and costume jewelry, bottles of essential oils, soap making kits, and enough makeup to keep a theatre company running for a decade. And that's just the garage.

The hall closet upstairs has soy candles and wax melts. My dad's walk-in closet in their master bedroom has been half taken over by leggings in every funky color and pattern you could imagine or never ask for, along with nail wraps to coordinate or clash, and even boxes of long-distance phone calling cards from some home business she ran decades ago. My mom is the undisputed MLM queen of the neighborhood. Maybe even the state. None of it has made her rich when you figure in all the time she's spent and all the profit she's funneled back into buying more products, so it's good my dad makes bank. All over the house are her ridiculous affirmation statements on post-it notes attached to the fridge, to bathroom mirrors, even on the corner of the TV screen, which is seriously beyond annoying. This week's batch includes:

Every day is another opportunity for success!

I am a confident, successful, and professional Network Marketer!

I now consciously and subconsciously flood every atom of my mind, body and soul with prosperity!

Yeah, that last one is a mouthful. So right now it's shakes and baked chicken breast and kale because we're *empowering our bodies to carry our best selves out into the world.*

"Well, are you coming on Sunday, or not?" she persists.

The last bite of chicken goes down.

"Not." I push to my feet, but Mom isn't ready to let it go.

"Blue."

"Mom." I answer her in the same flat tone she used on me.

"He's been there seven weeks and you haven't visited once— not even on Christmas! I don't think an afternoon is too much to give to your only brother."

"I'll get around to it." I refuse to let her guilt me into this. "Stop pushing."

Color floods her face. "What is wrong with you? Would it kill you to stop being so miserable and spend the day with your family?"

"Maybe it's my family that makes me miserable!" I snap, just as the front door opens and closes. My Dad gives us both a wary look as he walks into the kitchen.

"Is the food cold?" he asks, gesturing to the table. "Or did you two incinerate it shooting fire at each other?"

"I'll warm it up." Mom moves to the stove. "Blue can explain why she doesn't want anything to do with her brother—or us, apparently."

I roll my eyes. "Don't be so dramatic. I work on Sunday and I have a ton of homework."

She shoots me a look over her shoulder. "This early in the semester?"

Dad slouches tiredly into his chair at the table and reaches into his bag for his laptop. "You can't spare a couple of hours?" he asks me.

"It's a two hour drive up there," I remind him. "And then two hours back, plus the visit time."

He gives me a look that says he's not really buying my excuse but he'll let it ride. "Next time, then," he says, setting his laptop down on the table.

Mom makes a sound of disapproval as she sets a plate of food down next to the laptop. She'll probably unload on him after I'm out of hearing distance.

I make it to my room just as Jules FaceTimes me.

"Yo!" She calls out. I throw myself across the bed, rolling over to look at my phone.

"Thought you worked tonight."

"I'm here." She pulls the phone back to show me her surroundings. "Hank is mental today so I'm eating fries in the freezer."

"If he catches you on the phone, you're toast."

"Meh. He can't hear through the door. So—Allie B. told Lauren that Austin drove Maya home."

I try to sound unconcerned. "So?"

"So?" She repeats back. "He's ghosting you again, and now he's all up on her, of all people?"

"He's not ghosting me. We stopped talking a while ago."

Jules isn't fooled. "Thought you texted him last Friday?"

"It was nothing," I snap. "We're not like that anymore and it's fine. I don't need you going around telling everybody we're together when we're not."

"I'm not saying a thing!" Jules protests. "You were the one talking about him just the other day."

"Well, I'm not now. I'm not talking about him or Maya—at all. Got it?"

"Fine. Whatever." Jules is clearly pissed I don't want to rant about this with her. "Go be miserable. I gotta work."

She cuts me off before I can formulate a snappy comeback. That's twice in ten minutes I've been called miserable and who the hell could blame me if I am? I swear, everybody is out to make me that way.

Okay, I *am* miserable. I know I'm wallowing. But I really don't need the reminder of how lousy everything is in my life right now.

My brother's possible negligence got him incarcerated and killed a guy. *Check.*

My sort-of boyfriend is trying to hook up with the girl who hates me. *Check.*

The girl who hates me raised her hand in class today during a discussion about government action and the opiate epidemic to say that alcoholism is just as rampant and it kills people, too—and she gave me a pointed look that everyone saw. *Check.*

My parents tried to serve me guilt for dinner, along with kale. *Check.*

My best friend is determined to milk my rotten life for her own entertainment. *Check.*

I catch sight of my miserable face in the mirror over my dresser. Twenty minutes of every morning is spent straightening my dark hair to a sleek, beautiful shine, but you'd never know it now. My natural curl is sending it in various directions, making me look frayed. My eyes are more gray than blue, matching my mood, and my face is splotchy with residual anger. And hanging over my head in the reflection is yet another post-it note affirmation, courtesy of Mom the Boss Babe.

I roll off the bed and yank the note down, flipping it over my shoulder before I dig in my backpack for my copy of *Fahrenheit 451*. Might as well get started on it. Who knows, maybe I'll like it and memorize it. Although, there are other titles that might work better as my story. *Misery* comes to mind. Is *Drag Me To Hell* in book form, along with the movie? That would work.

Devon the unflappable new guy might have an inner book filled with rainbow-farting unicorns, but mine is frizzy hair, spirulina shakes and jailed family members. It's like memorizing an endless bad reality show. But hey, I made it through today. It'll get better, right?

My phone lights up with a text from Lauren, making sure I heard from Jules about what Allie B told her about Austin and Maya.

Flipping the covers over the phone as I open the book, my eyes stray to a bit of yellow on the carpet—the post-it note affirmation from Mom.

My story begins with this beautiful day.

Right.

IT DOESN'T GET any easier on day two. We were having a discussion about personal observations in Political Science and the definition of child abuse. Is a parent screaming at their child on the playground being abusive? Or are they just having a hard day and you're seeing a bad moment? What if they were yelling at their child out of fear for their safety? Mr. Jones was trying to get us all to examine the variables of social norms and discuss the difficulties and nuances of trying to judge behavior without context. At least that's how it was supposed to be.

Instead, Maya brought up a point about privilege and assumptions of privilege and how they play into the narrative of child abuse. "For instance," she said, "wealthy parents might be perceived as better parents due to their privilege, when they're really neglecting their kids. The kids can become reckless and feel like they can get away with anything—maybe even killing someone."

She said it very innocently, and Mr. Jones sputtered a bit before he told her it was an interesting point. He totally missed the Cheshire Cat smile that followed the remark. The kind of smile that makes you wonder if there are fangs behind those lips.

And of course, this was after I spent lunch once again listening to Devon chatter his sunshine and lollipops while I tried not to stare at Austin and Maya. They didn't look like they were *together* together exactly, but they were awfully friendly. Nobody seems to know just what they are to each other, which isn't surprising because Austin is really good about not being particularly anything to anyone—at least that's my experience.

I have a shift at BurgerMania right after school so I don't have to go home and deal with my mom in my face again. I'm restocking the cups when a familiar powder-blue VW Bug pulls up to the drive-thru.

"Really?" I ask as he rolls down his window. "Triple bacon cheeseburger and a side of cheese fries with a milkshake? Do you want to die young?"

Devon stares up at me for a moment and then breaks into his easy grin. "A guy's got to eat," he says. "I signed up to run a 5k in the fall, so I have to start building muscle mass."

"You're a runner?"

"Nope. Trying something new."

"I'm pretty sure you need clear arteries for that kind of activity. Does your mom know you eat like this?"

He shrugs. "I'm on my own for dinner most times."

"You need anything else?" I ask, taking his money and giving him the change. "There's ketchup and salt in the bag."

"Got a burger, got to see you," he says. "I'm good."

"You just saw me at lunch."

"That was an entire meal ago."

I wave him off. "Enjoy your heart attack."

"Will do." He waves back before the Bug zooms off. Jules comes up over my shoulder.

"That the new guy?" She asks "The stalker from the playground?"

"That's him," I nod. "His name is Devon."

"I know his name, buttmunch. I just didn't get a good look at him in the car, is all. So is he hot for you?"

"I don't think so. I'm just one of the first people he talked to and he lives in the neighborhood so he sort-of latched onto me."

"And you latched right back because Austin's jerking you around," she notes.

I don't like the picture she's painting. "I'm only being nice."

"I'm just saying—he's not hard on the eyes and everybody's going to start noticing him once you and Maya aren't news anymore." She shrugs. "Nobody knows anything about him. He says he comes from somewhere in Florida?"

"Yeah, I think." I answer. "I don't know that much about him." That might be because I'm trying to look like I'm talking to somebody other than Austin, but the fact is I haven't asked Devon much about himself. I feel kind of bad about it, now that I realize it.

"Well, get the deets as soon as you can. People want to know," Jules tells me.

The drive-thru bell chimes again and I tap my headset, waving Jules back to the back counter where she's supposed to be pulling orders. We work steadily for the next ninety minutes or so and I'm glad because it takes my mind off of everything. My world turns into bagging orders, pouring drinks, taking money and handing change out of the window, mind-numbing and perfect.

It was too good to last, of course. I know his voice the minute it comes through the speaker.

Austin.

He pulls up to the window and I let out a breath when I see he's alone. He at least manages to look a little guilty when the window opens and he sees it's me.

"Hey," he says.

"Hey," I answer flatly—like he's just another customer. "It's $8.28."

He puts his debit card into my palm. A brief fantasy scenario plays in my head where I take off running to my car, floor the gas pedal and go straight to the mall, where I clean out his bank account buying a closet full of shoes and an entire skin care line at Ulta. He forgets he told me his pin number is his football jersey number repeated twice. The card is swiped and handed back along with his food.

"See you," he says, not bothering to make anything further in the way of conversation. I should probably be grateful for that—it would have only been awkward and really uncomfortable—but I'm still stung by it. I didn't even know he knew who Maya was before they started hanging. I mean, it's a small school, so of course he knew Maya, and after everything with Jack and the accident, everybody knew Maya. But she wasn't somebody that Austin hung out with before. It makes me wonder why he suddenly sought her out now.

My mind chews that over and over as the dinner rush winds down. Hank, my manager, is in the back stockroom, so I walk across to Jules, poke her in the ribs from behind and laugh as she jumps.

"What the f—" she stops herself before she says a word in front of customers that would get her in trouble.

"Do you have English Lit this semester?" I ask her.

"I had it last semester," she says. "I had to read *1984*, remember?"

"You mean you watched the movie and skimmed the Wikipedia article."

"Works for me," she shrugs. "Want to borrow my paper so you can fudge it up a little and make it your own?"

34

"We wouldn't get away with that. Besides, Linza's got us reading *Fahrenheit 451*. It's about people who memorize books because the government outlaws them."

"Who could memorize a book?" she asks, wide-eyed.

"Depends on how big the book is. I have to pick a book to give my presentation on. What would you pick to memorize?"

She rolls her eyes. "I'd pick *Fifty Shades of Grey*. All those middle-aged ladies paying me just to hear a few pages of my story," she says, waving her hand as if seeing it unfold in front of her. "They'd be driving me around like my personal chauffeurs just so they can get an hour of read time in. And I'd make it worth their while—lots of moans and grunts and heavy breathing."

I laugh at the mental picture, then check to be sure Hank isn't going to come up from the back room and bust us for not working hard enough.

"Austin came through."

Jules blinks like an owl as my words come out of nowhere. "Was he alone?"

"Yeah. Whatever. I don't care what he does."

"Then why are you talking about him?"

"I guess I'm trying to figure out how he and Maya fit together," I say. "It's not like they used to hang out or anything. I mean, they barely knew each other."

"Didn't I tell you?" Jules shoves a french fry in her mouth. "Haylee told Other Julia that Maya started following Austin on Instagram. Then a week before the semester starts she went back and liked all of his pics in one night. Then she sends him a message to ask him about the football program at Audubon because her cousin is interested. That's how they started talking."

My drive-through bell rings and is ignored for a second as I pull my phone out and scroll back through Instagram. Just after break started I posted a pic of me and Austin taken at a local carnival back in the fall. Austin hadn't texted me for a few days when I posted it, and even though we were supposed to get together over break to hang out he still hadn't found the time. I was feeling needy and put the pic up with the caption: *Can't wait to do it all again.*

Maya must have realized he and I were together after that pic and made her move.

A voice calls through my headset.

"Uh . . . hello?"

I turn on my mic. "Sorry. Can I take your order?"

I rush back toward the window but I know Jules saw me looking at my phone. Why hadn't she let me know what Other Julia had told her before now? Probably because I bit her head off for being in my business earlier. But this is one of those times when you really should let your friend know what's going on.

It's clear Maya has drawn a target on me and she's determined to take me down one piece at a time—with Austin, with my classes—wherever she can. She's trying to destroy my life the way hers was destroyed. She can't get to Jack, so she's going through me. And if I fight back I'm the one who's going to look like the asshole because she's the one with the dead father.

I hand the next order out the window, fuming over the unfairness of it all. Part of me wonders if Austin should be warned that he's being used, but he deserves it. I throw myself back into work again, mindlessly cleaning counters, scrubbing down every inch of chrome on the shake machine and even meticulously wiping down the grate on the soda fountain tray. Hank pronounces me employee of the year as my drive-thru station positively sparkles by the time my shift is over. I smell like bleach and grease and my hair is back to being a frazzled mess again.

I wave my mom off in the living room later as she tries to engage me in conversation, insisting that I'm tired. After a shower, I sink down on my bed and mindlessly scroll through my phone. I'm on my fourth YouTube reaction video when the text comes through.

Hey

Oh, so now he wants to talk? Austin Bradley, you've got some balls. I really don't know what to say.

Hey

r u mad at me

As if I would give him the satisfaction.

No

Why

Maya

I'm tempted to ask *who*? But that would be way too obvious.

Are you guys
together now?

Does it bother you?

He didn't answer my question. Why should I answer his? I do, though.

> Do what you want

> She's a good person

I'm trying to think of an answer to that when he follows up with:

> and I need a good person in my life

What the hell is that supposed to mean?

> And I'm not???

> Don't be mad because people like her better than you

I stare at my phone open-mouthed. Where the hell is this coming from? It's not like he and I had a fight. We only ended because he stopped talking to me. And she's a *good person*? Since when does he even talk like that? Austin is a simple single-celled creature. He likes to eat, he likes to play football, he likes to drive his car, he likes Xbox. He wants to have sex with hot girls and he wants to smoke weed and he whines because doesn't get to do enough of those last two things. There's no way Austin would be pining for a *good person* in his life. How did she get into his head like this? I'm not going to bother addressing that in a text.

> I have to go

I shove the phone under my pillow, but it doesn't buzz again.

ON WEDNESDAY, MAYA told Haylee, who told Allie B, who told Jules, who told me that somebody heard me crying in the bathroom over Austin. I was not.

On Thursday, we had a discussion in Political Science about the early American colonies, and the development of social norms, standards, and laws. That somehow got railroaded into a discussion about how laws don't apply equally to all or get ignored entirely when rich people are able to buy the best lawyers.

On Friday night, Maya came into BurgerMania with Austin ten minutes before closing, and they stayed almost half an hour. I was on dining room, so I had to sweep—and sweep again as she kept dropping fries on the floor on her way out. Austin looked apologetic, but not enough to dump her since it's Monday again and according to his Instagram and her blowing up Snapchat all weekend, they're still together.

Austin tries to get my attention in the hall just as lunch starts, but I am not playing. I turn and walk the opposite way, planning to go into the cafeteria through the doors at the far end of the hall.

It's not long before I hear his quickening steps and feel his hand settle on my shoulder.

"Hey," he says.

"Yes?" I raise my eyebrows as I turn and give him my best bitch look right down the end of my nose.

"Uh..." He rubs a hand against the back of his neck. "Look," he says. "I...uh..." He looks down at the floor for a moment and then forces his eyes back to me. "This is awkward."

My eyebrows remain raised and I keep staring the dotted bitch line right through him. Let him feel awkward. He should feel awkward.

"About Maya..." He starts.

"I really couldn't care less."

"I just—it just happened. I mean you and me haven't really been hanging lately and—"

"Exactly." I cut him off sharply. "Are we done here?"

"I just feel bad, I guess," he has the nerve to say. "Maya and me just started talking and it kind of—well it went from there. But I want you to know I still think about you a lot."

"Is there a reason you're telling me this?"

"Yeah." He looks over his shoulder, as if he's making sure we're not overheard. "I just—I think about you a lot."

"You said that."

"And I'm not really sure what this thing is with Maya. It's almost like she's using me or something."

"Ya think?" I snap. "Wait a minute? What happened to *she's a good person and I need her in my life?*"

"What?" He looks at me in confusion.

"Tuesday. When you texted me."

His forehead crinkles up. "I didn't text you on Tuesday."

I whip out my phone and pull up the text, shoving it in front of his face. "I'm not hallucinating," I tell him.

He reads through the texts and his frown deepens. "Blue, that wasn't me."

"It's your phone number," I remind him.

He lets out an exaggerated breath. "It was Maya. I caught her going through my phone. We fought about it. I thought she was just jealous and trying to see who else I was texting. I didn't realize she was playing you like that."

That bitch! I should have realized.

"Well, now you know," I snarl. "You might want to think about what kind of girl you're with."

"We're not really exclusive," he assures me quickly.

"So?"

"So I'm just saying if you ever want to hang out—or are you with that new guy?"

I manage to shrug. "Not sure yet."

"Well, the offer's there." He looks over his shoulder again. "Text you later."

And with that he turns and strides off. He's that absolutely sure that I'm okay with him texting me later. That cocky, ridiculous asshat! As if I'm sitting around waiting for him to notice me again. And what? He's playing us both now?

I'm tempted to run after him just so I can spin him around by his shoulder and slap his face.

But I have to admit I am also equally intrigued by the idea of texting him tonight and maybe hanging out. Does Maya have a job? Maybe he and I can make a road trip. I still can't believe she played me and I fell for it.

She was checking up on him because it would piss her off blind if she knew we were texting each other. From the way Austin is talking, it sounds like he's just as vague with her as he is with all of his relationships. Maybe they have a thing and maybe he's just taking advantage of her trying to use him. They're using each other.

My internal monologue is interrupted by the jolt of an elbow into my side.

"Deep thoughts, huh?"

Devon's face is entirely too close as he leans in to mumble in my ear. I rear back, my nose crinkling.

"Dude, lose the onions."

He breathes hard into his cupped hand. "Sorry. It's Burger Bar today and I love my onions. I was just coming to find you."

"You don't need me to eat lunch with if you've already snarfed a burger."

"That was just my first burger," he says. "I could eat another two or five."

My eyes can't seem to help but look him up and down. How did I not notice before that he's in pretty good shape? He's got a lot more muscle on his arms and chest than I've paid attention to. If he raised that shirt there could be something close to a six pack underneath it.

"Keep it up and that hot bod is going to turn to flab," I warn.

His eyes light up. "You think I've got a hot bod?"

"Don't get all full of yourself. It's not the only bod in the school."

"Is that your way of letting me know you and lover-boy are back on again? With your *whatever*?"

I make a disgusted sound, not even dignifying that with a response and stomp off into the cafeteria. Devon follows and loads up with another burger and an extra-large order of baked crinkle fries. There's a salad on my plate, but it's completely subverted with a chocolate muffin and two chocolate chip cookies.

"So?" He presses. "You back with Austin or what?"

"No, I am not back with Austin. But it sounds like he wants to be back with me," I add, just in case Devon's got loose lips.

I'd love for that to get back to Maya. Now that I think about it, I should probably be telling Jules or other Julia. One of them is sure to let that slip in front of Haylee or Maya.

I glance around the cafeteria as casually as I can, looking to see if Maya and Austin are sitting together as usual. It's a pleasant surprise to see Maya and Haylee in the corner totally absorbed by their phones. Austin is not in sight.

"He's not over there," Devon says, tossing a fry into his mouth. "I can look for you so it doesn't seem so obvious."

"I'm not being obvious," I retort, even though I obviously am.

"You need to stop obsessing about her so much," he says to me. "Whatever it is she's trying to torment you with, you're playing right into it."

"You think she's trying to torment me?" That makes me feel good for some reason—like I'm not just imagining all this stuff.

"Doesn't matter what I think," Devon says. "*You* think she's tormenting you. And from your point of view, that's what matters."

I glance back over at Maya and Haylee again.

"Looks like there's trouble in lover town," I say. Maybe I can turn the screws a little.

Devon shakes his head. "Playing right in . . ."

"Are you going to turn all 'teacher' on me and tell me that the best thing I can do is ignore her? I've been to all the anti-bullying assemblies, thanks."

"How much rent are you charging her? Because that girl is living in your head."

"What do you know about it?" I snap. "Have you been through what I've been through? Dealing with a situation that upturned everything? Something that isn't your fault in any way but totally trashes your whole life?"

He goes still. Then he pauses a moment before he chooses his words.

"I'm not living your life. That doesn't mean I'm wrong. You can't change her actions—or the situation you were thrown into—but you can decide how you're going to react to all of this. Rattling her cage is only going to keep it going."

He's putting his burger together painstakingly and I finally pay attention to him enough to realize why. His hand is wrapped in an Ace bandage, and it's bulky in places, like there are gauze bandages under it on his knuckles and fingers. Spots of blood have soaked through the bandage in places.

"What happened to your hand?" I ask.

"Maybe I punched a slide," he mimes it with his good hand.

"Seriously. Did you fall skateboarding or something?"

He smiles. "Do I look like I skateboard?"

"You kind of have that careless skater boi hair," I point out. "And the hot bod."

His smile gets wider. "I do skateboard but I haven't done it lately. This was just a moment of idiocy. Nothing a whole lot of onions won't fix." He punctuates this by loading a layer of onions on to his burger thick enough to double it in size.

"You stay on that side of the table," I warn. "You just about melted my mascara off with that last blast."

"Consider it a lesson, my child," he says in a monotonous, sing-song voice. "If you eat a lot of onions, your enemies will avoid you."

As if sensing us from across the cafeteria, Maya looks up from her phone. We lock eyes and she gives me a wide cat-like grin, like I'm her favorite mouse and she just spied me stepping out of a hole in the wall. Her fingers fly over her phone. Maybe she's texting about me. Maybe she's posting about me. Whatever it is she definitely wants me to know it's about me.

Devon's hand closes over mine as it reaches for my phone. It's surprisingly warm and his thumb strokes the back of my hand.

"Don't do it. She's watching you and she wants you to do it."

44

He's right, but it pisses me off that he is. I already have her manipulating me. I don't need him telling me what to do, too.

"I was just seeing what time it was," I say, standing up with my tray. "I need to get to my next class early. There's a presentation due and I want to look it over first."

He smiles and nods, even though his face says he doesn't believe me.

"Later," he says. "Hope there's room in your head for that presentation. You might have to ask Maya to move all the baggage you're letting her keep there."

"Eat your onions."

"Onions are love," he pulls a long string of onion off his burger and slurps it down. "Onions are life."

I shake my head as I walk away, and of course, I barely make it to the hallway before I'm on my phone, checking. Her story features a pic of Devon in the cafeteria. I'm sitting across from him, and it was just taken because she's zoomed in on his injured hand so much that I'm barely visible in the shot.

Better warn a brutha, she captioned it. *Hanging with certain people can leave you injured or dead.*

My face flushes hot red with anger and then deepens to crimson as Maya strolls past, a smirk on her lips.

I have a vivid mental picture of me rushing up behind her and shoving her hard into the wall until that smirk meets concrete. But then everyone would stop to pick her up and console her because she lost her dad and I only lost my previously peaceful life. I'd be the asshole. Not her. Never her.

How long am I going to have to put up with this? How long do I have to be the bigger person?

I'm not the bigger person. I'm small. And petty. And mean. And I have a presentation due in two minutes with all of this on my mind.

I can hear Devon's voice in my head telling me to find my inner rainbow or something. I could start repeating some of my mom's inspirational post-it notes. He'd probably like that. He could choke down a stack of them, covered in onions.

Despite my black mood, that mental picture makes me smile. Just a little.

Okay Devon, I think. *I'll embrace my inner onion and just get through this presentation. That's all I have to do.*

I WAIT UNTIL the last possible minute to go into Poly Sci because I know if I'm sitting there too long, and Maya even looks at me sideways, I'm going to snap and say something to her.

She's unbelievable. Stealing Austin's phone just so she can get to me! Using him like that.

No matter how tempting it is, I'm not going to text him. That would make me as bad as she is, using him to get back at her. I will not give either of them the satisfaction. But it is really, really tempting.

And that pic she posted of Devon—my stomach tightens just thinking about it.

I slip into the room right behind Mr. Jones, and go straight to my desk. Luckily, I sit three rows in front of Maya, so I don't have to look at her smirking face. Her eyes are boring into me, though. Let her look. She's probably wishing she could be with Austin because he genuinely liked her. The way he genuinely likes me. Not that I want him, but it gives me some small satisfaction to know that they're only together because she's using him. And he's letting her.

They're disgusting.

Guilt pricks me and anger flares again over it. I can't even be properly pissed at her. She thinks my brother killed her father. In her place, I'd probably feel the same. I wouldn't go to the lengths she's going to in an effort to make her life miserable, though. At least, I don't think I would.

She's grieving. I get it. Grief processes differently for everyone. Hating me is a lot easier than mourning her father. She's being petty and vindictive, but that's how she's processing.

I can be the bigger person. I can.

By the time Mr. Jones calls up the first presenter, my blood pressure is down and I'm in a much better place mentally.

We have been studying the Civil Rights Act of 1964 in class this week. The presentation today involves each of us reading a two hundred word letter that we've written from the viewpoint of someone living at that time, and how they feel the Civil Rights Act will impact their lives. We had to draw papers from a bowl, with each of us getting someone from a different profession or a different station in life. I got a teacher in a soon-to be desegregated white school.

My letter was all about how excited I was to finally have the kids in my class integrated and being taught equally, and that I was hopeful there would be more programs to help some of the more economically challenged children.

"Nicely done, Blue," Mr. Jones says. "Although it took years for many of those affirmative action programs to click in, the Civil Rights Act was a good first step toward getting us there."

"Affirmative Action programs like scholarships?" Maya asks. "Like scholarships offered to kids to get them into Audubon Academy?"

Mr. Jones shrugs. "The Academy scholarships aren't entirely based on financial need, or based specifically on ethnic diversity, but those are certainly factors that go into the deliberations."

"So of course, Blue wants to be the teacher who feels like she's a good person just for doing what the school should have been doing all along."

My temper instantly ignites. "That's not what I said!"

"That's what it sounded like to me. Sounded like a teacher trying to play like they're being a good person. Or a student trying to pretend to be a good person by writing a cheesy letter about being a good person."

"Maya—" Mr. Jones begins to warn.

"Don't put words in my mouth!" I shoot back. "In fact, you can keep my name out of your mouth entirely."

"Girls!" Mr. Jones cuts in again.

"You got a problem with me all you've got to do is say so." Maya says, standing up.

"I'm not the one with the problem," I retort. "Maybe you don't recognize someone being a good person because you're out of practice."

"At least my family members aren't driving people off the road!" She snarls.

"At least I don't have to break into my boyfriend's phone because I'm worried that he's texting girls that he'd rather be talking to!" I shoot back.

"All right, let's just calm down here!" Mr. Jones exclaims.

"Bitch!" Maya shrieks.

Mr. Jones turns to reprimand her just as I let out the word—the "C" word—and the entire class gasps.

"Girls!" Mr. Jones thunders. "Out! Both of you in the hall now!"

I wait for Maya to walk through the door first. No way am I turning my back to her. Mr. Jones gets between us and I follow him out. Once we're in the hallway, he turns and shuts the door.

"Office time. Let's go." He starts walking and it finally sinks in that I've really done it now. I shoot Maya a look that is nothing but pure hatred and she returns it tenfold as we trail behind him.

Once we get there, Mrs. Logan, the assistant principal, ushers us into her office and closes the door.

Mr. Jones makes the whole thing sound a lot worse than it really was. The way he tells it, blood was spraying and we were lobbing grenades at each other. Maya and I sit in stony silence. My arms are folded across my chest, my legs are crossed, and my foot is swinging madly. I look over at Maya and realize we're doing the exact same thing, so I change my position.

"I'll be emailing your parents about today," Mrs. Logan informs us both.

I bite my lip and stare at the carpet, but Maya, the perpetual victim, starts going off.

"Mrs. Logan, she started this," she fumes. "She's been harassing me since the day I got back! She wrote that presentation just to pick on me because I'm a scholarship student. She's a bully and we have a school policy about that."

My mouth drops open.

"Are you kidding me? *I'm* harassing *you*??" I can't believe she has the nerve to even say it. "I've been putting up with your nasty posts and all the rotten remarks you've been making in class and behind my back!"

"Enough!" Mrs. Logan holds up a hand. "Girls, we all know that you both faced a very difficult situation last year. No one is expecting you to be best friends, but we do expect you to treat each other with respect while on this campus."

I make a snorting sound and Maya *tsks* her tongue to her teeth, both of us making it clear what we think of that statement.

"It might be best if we bring Mrs. Ramsey in on this," Mr. Jones suggests. "You know me, I'm not so great with the girl drama. And I need to get back to class."

Mrs. Logan taps a finger to her chin. "Thank you, Mr. Jones. And I do think Mrs. Ramsey is a good idea, under the circumstances."

I roll my eyes mentally. Ugh. Mrs. Ramsey is the school counselor. I have a feeling my mom will be emailed a list of anger management counselors in the area. Lucky for me she just started selling essential oils. She'll have me dabbing bergamot and lavender on my wrists instead.

"After I email both of your parents," Mrs. Logan goes on, "you can expect after-school detention."

"But I have work!" I protest.

"And I have basketball," says Maya.

"Your school obligations come first," Mrs. Logan reminds us. "Perhaps next time you'll consider the repercussions before you act irresponsibly. Tomorrow, you're going to spend some time after school figuring out how to get along with each other."

Maya's eyes lock with mine. Tomorrow we're going to spend some time after school figuring out how to keep Maya from splattering me against a wall.

Maybe my mom has an essential oil for that.

9

"YOU'RE NOT TAKING this seriously."

My mother has gone into full hoverparent mode. The TV is off. We're sitting at the kitchen table, carefully set with the notepad that recorded her thoughts on the email from Mrs. Logan, and two cups of chamomile tea. She even lit her serenity candle. God help me.

"Mom—" I begin carefully.

"What has gotten into you, Blue? You used to be such a good student."

"I *am* a good student," I remind her. "My GPA is doing just fine."

"That's not what I'm talking about, and you know it," she retorts. "We're discussing your school experience. The interactions that shape and enhance your daily life."

"You mean like this one?" I cross my arms. "Not feeling too enhanced."

Her face turns crimson with anger, but she doesn't raise her voice. It's not her style.

"I just want you to acknowledge the gravity of the situation. You were completely out of line," she insists.

"It was one little disagreement that's being totally blown out of proportion," I retort. "If they'd just move us to separate classes, Maya and I wouldn't have to deal with each other."

"I've already requested that," Mom says. "But Audubon isn't that large. Even if you don't have a class together again, you'll still see each other in the halls or at lunch. The two of you are going to have to learn how to deal with each other."

"You can't just lock us in a room together after school and expect us to be buddies."

Mom raises a brow. "Mrs. Ramsey is a licensed counselor and I'm sure she's dealt with harder cases than you."

"So I'm stuck losing hours at work so I can sit in a desk next to Maya and write essays about conflict resolution and communication skills? How is that a good use of anybody's time?"

I glare into my tea mug. I hate chamomile tea. It tastes like weeds you'd pull out of the backyard. It's not soothing at all. I have a brief fantasy of pouring my tea all over mom's lavender verbena serenity candle. Strangely, the mental image helps, so I guess chamomile is soothing after all.

Mom taps a perfectly manicured finger—complete with the custom nail wrap design that's on sale this month—on the table.

"You know," she says, "when I'm faced with challenges or objections, I try to take a step back and ask myself: what's the lesson here?" Her hands move elegantly as she falls into one of her marketing presentations. "What's the takeaway—and how do we use this to energize our authentic selves into forward motion?"

My eyes roll hard enough that I can feel them bouncing against the back of my skull.

"Save it, please. I'm not selling Maya any diet shakes."

"You're not even listening to what I'm trying to get across—" Mom starts, but I interrupt.

"Are we done?"

She lets out a sigh, then takes a lengthy pull of her chamomile tea. "You're excused," she says, waving me off. She'll probably grab a wineglass as soon as I clear the doorway.

I stomp down the hallway, grabbing my coat out of the hall closet.

"You're not taking the car anywhere but work and school for a week," she calls out.

"I'm going for a walk," I snarl and slam out the door.

I am still so angry I vibrate with it. This is all so freaking unfair. I'm getting all the fallout for this when hardly anything I did deserved it.

Tears burn my eyes as I walk briskly through the neighborhood. I'm so furious, it takes me a minute to realize it's snowing heavily. The playground is deserted, of course, so I let myself in through the gate on the chain link fence. The slide has a layer of snow over it, which I brush off before I climb the platform and lay down, with my feet dangling down the slide, feeling the cold plastic through the thin layer of my jeans.

I need to come up with a warmer place to be alone with my thoughts. Most teenage girls would just go to their room, but they don't live with my mother. If she heard so much as a sniffle from behind my closed door, she'd be busting in with an essential oil diffuser, a gratitude journal, and more freaking chamomile tea.

I swipe the angry tears from my eyes, refusing to cry over this. It really pisses me off when I get angry enough to cry. Guys don't do that stuff—they just hit things. The crack is still there on the slide where my fist connected. It didn't make me feel any better then, and repeating it wouldn't make me feel any better now.

The snow is really coming down, and my ears soak in the delicious quiet that comes with it. Everything is so still and the air is cold and fresh. I pull it in through my nose, breathing it out slowly from my mouth, repeating the action for a long time—until I can't feel my face anymore. Maybe I should take up meditation. I'm sure Mom has plenty of mantras I can recite to myself over and over.

My phone vibrates. Probably Jules, or Mom wanting to know where the hell I am, I've been gone so long. I'm debating whether or not to look at it when someone opens the gate to the playground.

It's Devon. I know that beanie anywhere. He's got his head down, so he doesn't see me wave. I'm about to call out to him when walks over, knocks the snow off one of the swings, and sits down. His shoulders slump, and he faces away from the gate, staring at the ground. His hands wrap around the chains on each side, and one foot pushes him slowly back and forth, back and forth.

Devon takes a deep, shuddering breath so loud I can hear it from here. I feel like I'm spying on a private moment, and pull myself a little further down the slide so that I'm blocked by the low wall around the platform. Only my eyes look over.

Back and forth, back and forth. He removes his hand from the chain, and rubs it across his nose, lifting his head to do so.

Is he crying? I think he might be crying.

I am intruding horribly. Part of me feels like I should let him know I'm here—if only to offer a shoulder if he needs it. God knows he's been my sounding board for a while now. But what if he's embarrassed instead? Or worse—really pissed at me for spying on him?

I'm reminded that we met in this exact circumstance and he was spying on *me*.

I should go over to him. I should let him know I'm here and then he can decide if he wants to talk to me or tell me to mind my own business.

What if he tells me to mind my own business?

I'm overthinking this. I'm going sit up and call his name, but just as I start to, he stands up. I chicken out and shrink back down again with my eyes barely above the edge of the slide. Devon takes in another long breath, stretching out his legs and shaking his arms as if he's putting feeling back into them. He cradles his injured hand, rubbing it lightly to get it warm.

Finally, he walks over and lets himself out the gate, and I watch him go, berating myself for not saying something. Even if he had known I was there, he clearly didn't want to talk to anyone. Still, he looked like he needed a friend, and God knows I could really use one, too. One who doesn't talk behind my back. One who isn't in jail.

I really want to know what Devon is going through. Whatever it is has broken through his sunny exterior and done some damage.

It occurs to me again that I don't know him, really. There's a pang in my stomach at the thought. I've been so busy dealing with all my crap and he never seems to be bothered by anything. Maybe he's just better at dealing with things than I am.

Or maybe that's just what he wants everyone to think.

No one gets to read my book, he'd said, *not until I kill the villain.*

What did he mean by that? What sort of villain does he have in his life? Mine roams the halls and stalks me all over social media, standing behind a victim shield that I don't dare hurl anything against. Devon's villain is hiding in the shadows, painted over with a layer of sunshine and rainbows.

Something about that makes me feel even colder, and I watch the snow swirl around him until he's just a blur, fading into the darkness.

DEVON WASN'T IN first block today, or at lunch. He must be out sick. Only, he didn't look sick last night. Heartsick, maybe. Maybe he took a mental health day, to deal with whatever he's dealing with. I've needed mental health days every so often. Believe it or not, Mom is fine with it every time I do. She makes me chamomile tea and talks to me about the importance of hydration and proper sleep. I don't do it very often, mostly because by the end of the day she's driven me completely insane.

So yeah, he's probably just taking a mental health day. Which is a good thing.

Unless you look as sad as he did last night. The memory of his tears and his drooping shoulders pulls at me, and I have a hard time concentrating all day because of it. I mean, he barely knows anybody here, other than me. At least, I've never seen him hang out with anybody. Maybe that's why he was sad—he misses his friends back in Florida. Maybe he hates it here. Maybe he left a girl behind.

That thought slides from my head right down into my gut with a hollow clang. Not that I'm crushing on him or anything. I know people are talking because we sit together at lunch every day, but he's a good friend. He's a really good friend. I just don't like to think about him being lonely, and missing some girl.

Some girl who's probably pretty, and laughs a lot, and isn't so damn miserable all the time.

I catch Jules in the hall between third and fourth block.

"Hey, was Devon in class today?" I ask her.

"Florida man? Nah, he's out today."

I frown at the use of her new nickname for him. "Oh. Okay." I shrug like it was nothing, but she's not going to let it go.

"Why—you missing him?"

"I borrowed his pen. I need to get it back to him."

"It's a pen."

"It's his favorite. It's got a really smooth roller." It's all I can think of, but she buys it.

"You should keep it, then."

"I'll just give it to him when he comes back."

"Or, you could drop it by his house," she suggests. "He lives over on Willow Court."

"I know that. And it can wait."

"If you change your mind and go, let me know what his house looks like inside." She pushes open the door to a nearby bathroom and steps inside. I follow her.

"What is *that* supposed to mean?"

"Dude, I've got to pee." She tosses her backpack at my feet and steps into a stall.

I bend over to look under the other two stalls. "Nobody else is in here and I've heard you pee before. What makes you think I'm going to see something crazy if I go to his house?"

"Word around the neighborhood is that his family is antisocial." She raises her voice so I can hear her over the peeing. "Like, his parents are almost never there, and when they are there, they barely talk to anybody. You remember Olivia Farrell?"

She flushes and then wipes her hands on me as she passes me on her way to the sink.

"Yuck! Jules!"

"Listen to me pee, pay the price," she says matter-of-factly.

I suppress a shudder and stick to the subject. "Is Olivia that girl on the bus that wore the hot pink rubber bands on her braces?"

"That's her," she confirms as she washes her hands. "The Princess chick with all the glitter. Her family lives next door to Devon and they went over to say hello right after they moved in. Olivia told me her mom said his parents both looked like they'd been dragged behind a truck. Bags under their eyes, didn't talk much. I just wondered if they had a meth lab in the basement."

"That's a rotten thing to say." I pick up her backpack and handed it to her. "Maybe they were just tired from unpacking boxes. Jesus, even the neighborhood loves to gossip."

"All the moms in the neighborhood gossip," Jules says. "You've seen enough home jewelry parties to know that."

"Since when did you become buddies with Olivia?"

"Since Olivia saw me at the movies and suddenly remembered that I went to Audubon," Jules says. "She wanted to know if I knew Devon."

"Oh she did, did she?" That comes out a lot harder than I intended. Jules gives me a knowing look.

"Come on, you had to notice he's hot."

"Of course, I noticed. And if she's stalking him, then talking smack about his family is probably not the best way to get his attention," I point out.

She shrugs. "Just passing along the info."

"He's probably got a girlfriend back in Florida."

Jules makes a non-committal sound as she reaches for the door, and I put my hand out to stop her.

"Does he?" I ask.

"How would I know?"

"You guys talk in second block—or so he tells me. I thought he might have mentioned it, is all."

"Nope. Gotta go." She opens the door and says over her shoulder, "Nice peeing for you. Perv."

Well, that conversation got me nowhere. I'm concerned about Devon. Not worried, exactly. Just . . . wondering. About lots of things.

I could drive by his house after school, if I knew which house it was. Or which house Olivia lives in, for reference. I could text Jules and ask, but that would only have her assuming things again.

It's a stupid idea. I've got detention after school, anyway.

My mood is not improved by that thought.

"ALL RIGHT, YOU two," Mrs. Ramsey says as she leans against her closed office door and stares us both down. "I knew there was a chance we'd end up in this room, but I was hoping you'd both take the high road." She levels a glance first at Maya and then over at me and I bristle inwardly at the fact that she's looking at both of us the same way. I didn't do that much. And I only did it in reaction to Maya but I'm the one getting strapped in and forced to take the ride with her.

"So who wants to go first?" Mrs. Ramsey asks. "And no interrupting each other. I need to know what's happening here from both points of view."

Maya stares at her belligerently and my face has the exact same expression.

"She was making fun of me in her presentation." Maya snaps.

"I was not!" I shoot back. "If you identified a little too closely, it's not my problem."

"Because my Dad didn't buy my way in here?" she retorts. "I had to *earn* my scholarship."

"Oh, please! Throwing down the scholarship card like it makes you something special!"

"You don't know a thing about me!"

"I know you like to make up relationships. Austin says you're not even together."

"That's a lie! You are so pathetically jealous!"

"Of you?" I laugh out loud. "Crayola doesn't even make your shade of crazy."

"Bitch!"

I only get the "F" sound of my reply out before Mrs. Ramsey cuts me off.

"Enough!" She takes a deep breath. "Blue, is it possible you were insensitive with your presentation—not considering it could have been perceived as being pointed at Maya?"

Maya is smiling that Cheshire Cat smile again. Why bother talking? Mrs. Ramsey's head swivels and she catches Maya with that smile on her face.

"And Maya," she continues, "Mr. Jones tells me that you have gone out of your way to make very pointed commentary during class discussions. Commentary that could easily be construed as being directed at Blue."

Oh. So Mr. Jones *did* notice. He didn't bother to do anything about it at the time, though.

Now it's Maya's turn to shut up. We both sit, bodies angled away from each other, arms folded across our chests, completely mute.

Mrs. Ramsey lets out a sigh and takes a seat behind her desk. She crosses her legs and loops her folded hands over one knee.

"All right," she says. "Nobody wants to talk about the elephant in the room. I understand how uncomfortable that must be for both of you. Maya lost her father. Blue, you lost your brother." She holds up a hand to stifle Maya's sputter of indignation before she goes on.

"Of course Blue's loss is nothing compared to yours, Maya, but it's a loss all the same. Her brother is incarcerated. Like you, her home life has been turned upside down. Both of your lives have been altered in very different ways, but what I'm getting at here is that there was impact to you both. For the moment, that fact and this high school are all that you have in common. Am I right?"

I glare sideways at Maya and the word *Austin* might as well be written across my face because she reads it easily and gives me a little smirk.

Mrs. Ramsey leans back in her chair, looking at me, then Maya, and then back at me again. "I want you both to reach into your backpacks and pull out some paper and a pen," she requests, motioning us both to move closer in to the desk so we can use our side of it for writing.

We both make a face, but we do what she asks. I set my pen down on my paper and look at her expectantly.

"Maya is right," Mrs. Ramsey says. "You don't know her. Not really."

I grit my teeth at the smug look on Maya's face.

"And she doesn't know you. So here's your first assignment," Mrs. Ramsey goes on. "I want you to write five things about the other person that make you completely different from each other."

"Five things like what?" Maya asks, giving me a look of pure loathing. "I could give you a book full of things."

"Yeah, kind of hard to pick just five," I agree.

"Well then, you've got plenty to choose from." Mrs. Ramsey smiles in a really annoying way. "It can be as simple as the difference in your eye color, or it can be as complex as describing your genetic code. I don't really care. Just give me five things that make you different from each other."

I look down at my paper. There's a serious urge to write paragraphs, but I want to get through this and get out of here as quickly as possible.

Number one, I write. *Maya has brown eyes.* At least I think she has brown eyes. I glance over quickly to make sure.

Number two: Maya plays basketball.

Number three: Maya is a scholarship recipient.

I scratch that out. She already made me sound like I made a big deal out of that.

Number three: Maya doesn't have an iPhone. Wait. Does that sound privileged? It might sound privileged. She's got me second-guessing myself. I scratch that out, too.

Number three: Maya has Biology for second block. I know because Alli B. has her in class.

Number four. Number four . . . Okay, I'm honestly getting stumped. *Number four: Maya doesn't have a car.* That probably sounds privileged again but I don't care anymore.

I glance over at her, and she is writing a freaking book on her paper, her hand flying across the page. I guess she wants to stay here all afternoon. Knowing her, she just wants *me* to stay here all afternoon, and she's willing to suck it up and stay herself if it means I'm stuck here, too. Spiteful bitch.

I scratch out number four and write *Maya thinks it's fun to deliberately insert herself into other people's lives and cause drama.* I look over again. She's still writing.

I go on. *Without a thought for the ripple effect of her actions, she targets other people with her bullying. She is petty and shallow and manipulative to the people around her who have the misfortune of considering her to be a friend.*

I look over at her again. It looks like she might have stopped writing. Okay, I'll wrap this up.

Number five: Maya's perfume smells like floor cleaner.

I set my pen down, and raise my eyebrows, giving Maya my best smug grin—only to find it staring me in the face as she does the same.

"All right," Mrs. Ramsey says, folding her hands on the desk in front of her. "Let's hear them. Who wants to go first?"

Neither of us speaks for a second and then Maya shrugs her shoulders. "I'll go. Whatever. Item one," she begins.

Item? She can't just say *number one* like a normal person?

"Blue has a stupid name and I would be embarrassed if I had a name like that. I don't know why she doesn't use a nickname or go by her middle name or something unless it's even more embarrassing than her first name, which is hard to imagine."

I grit my teeth because she's not wrong. My middle name is Antoinette, for my Italian grandmother on my father's side. I suppose I could go by Ann or Toni, but then I have to explain why I'm bypassing one name and shortening another, and it's just easier to suck it up and go with Blue.

"Very well," Mrs. Ramsey says, as if Maya has just put forward a thoughtfully constructed debate point. "Blue?"

"Number one," I read. "Maya has brown eyes."

I sound lame. I sound *so* lame. Like I can't have an original thought so I just did what Mrs. Ramsey suggested as an example.

"Well, that's certainly the most civilized response so far," Mrs. Ramsey says. "What's next on your list, Maya?"

"Blue doesn't know how to treat her boyfriends," she says in a sugary-sweet voice. "That's why they lose interest."

My hand tightens around my list so hard that I crinkle the paper.

"Blue do you have a second point you'd like to make?" Mrs. Ramsey asks coolly.

"Maya plays basketball. Badly." I add.

Maya makes a noise with her teeth and mumbles the word *jealous* under her breath.

"No commenting beyond reading your point, please," Mrs. Ramsey cautions. "Is that it for point two?"

I nod and she looks over at Maya. "Three?"

"Blue has a loved one with a drinking problem." Maya states flatly.

I suck in a breath but before I can start tearing into her, Mrs. Ramsey holds up a hand. "Maya, since you don't live in the same house as Blue, any conclusions on your part about her family members are mere conjecture."

"Not if there's a police report," Maya says, smiling sweetly.

"And the police report showed my brother was under the legal limit," I remind her. "But I guess facts don't play into this for you."

"Here's a fact for you!" Maya jams a finger toward my face. "My father was run off the road by your idiot brother who was probably drunk but had a better lawyer. Maybe he was reaching for his next beer when he took his eyes off the road."

"Maybe if your father hadn't been texting, he would have stayed on the road, and you'd be torturing him right now instead of me!" I snarl back.

"Girls!" Mrs. Ramsey stands up. "This isn't productive!"

She moves out of her chair and around her desk to get between us, but it's too late. Maya's on her feet and so am I. She pushes me hard in my chest, sending me backwards, stumbling into my chair. I catch myself before I fall, and whirl back around, still reeling. I lunge for Maya and end up falling into her instead, sending her into her own chair. Her legs tangle up in it and she falls, crashing to the floor.

She screams, but it's more a sound of rage than anything else.

"Maya!" Mrs. Ramsey rushes to her and Maya makes the most of it, rolling over and clutching her foot like I just chopped it off with an axe.

"Oh, come on," I sneer.

Mrs. Ramsey crouches on the floor and she puts a hand up as if to physically stop me from getting in there and finishing Maya off. I slump back down into my chair as she gets an arm around Maya's shoulders and helps her to her feet. Maya is moaning and hopping dramatically, doing her best to try to squeeze some fat crocodile tears out of her eyes but they won't come.

"I'm taking her to the nurse's office," Mrs. Ramsey snaps at me. "Wait here—I'll be calling your parents right after hers."

Outstanding. I wonder if there's a spirulina shake to counteract this event. My life just went from bad to worse, and I have a feeling it's all downhill from here.

"AND ANOTHER THING!" My mother fumes.

This is her fourth *and another thing* and it's about three more than I have the patience to hear.

"I don't think you realize how lucky you are, especially since this is a second offense," she says, sloshing her energizing smoothie out of her glass as she gestures.

"It wasn't as bad as everybody's making it sound," I grumble.

"You threw her to the ground!"

"She shoved me first!"

Mom sucks in a deep breath, shoves her manicured hand through her hair, shoots my Dad a look and goes on.

"They're willing to let you both off with a week of full suspension, followed by eight weeks of after-school detention since you and Maya are both honor students."

"And since you and Dad make significant donations to the school," I point out.

Mom pulls in another breath and closes her eyes as if she needs a minute to keep from screaming at me. Like she ever would. My mother is not a screamer. She's a salesperson. Right now she's trying to figure out how to turn this entire situation into a lesson for me that will yield a net result of me living my best, most radiant life because that's a win for her.

Dad, who has been sitting quietly all this time, letting her have the spotlight, clears his throat and finally speaks.

"Being a donor is a definite advantage in this situation," he agrees. "But you're not going to buy your way out of this. You're serving detention with the school counselor—and the Rodriguez girl."

"But I've got two AP classes!" I protest. "And a job."

"You're going to have to back off work. Realign your priorities," Mom says.

"We told you before to stay away from that girl," Dad reminds me. "Why don't you just avoid her? I should think you wouldn't want to stir anything up, anyway."

"She's been harassing me from the day she came back." I tell him miserably.

Dad's eyes narrow. "Make me a detailed list of everything—all the social media, all the comments in the hallway—anything else she's done to deliberately harass you."

"Why?"

"I assume the school has a bullying policy. If I get Hazleton and Farr involved, we may be able to get her removed."

I swallow hard. Hazleton and Farr is the law firm we have on retainer. "Like, get Maya expelled?"

"It doesn't have to be that ugly," Mom says, tapping a finger on the table as she muses. "I'm sure the school and her mother will come to some sort of understanding that doesn't reflect too badly on her record."

I shake my head and something in my stomach turns over. "Then everyone will just talk about how my parents and their lawyer ran Maya out of school. Just like they talk about how my parents and their lawyer got my brother out of a manslaughter charge."

Dad's mouth tightens into a thin line. "When you hear that sort of talk, you need to bring it to the teacher's attention."

"Absolutely." Mom nods her head. "We're not paying them good money to let gossip drag our family name through the dirt." She turns to Dad, puts a hand on his arm. "Maybe you should talk to Jerry."

"Davis?" Dad rubs his chin. "I supposed he could speak to the principal."

"Who's Jerry Davis?" I ask.

Mom waves a hand. "He's on the school board. He golfs with your father."

"Ugh. No." My voice comes out a little too loud. "Just let me deal with this, please."

"But you're *not* dealing with it," my mother points out.

"Stay out of it." The words come out through gritted teeth. "You'll only make things worse. Harder."

Mom raises her brows and turns her head to share a look with my father. He shrugs in return and she narrows her eyes at him, clearly hoping for a stronger response.

"Look." I let out a sigh. "You said we have to learn to deal with each other. So let us do that. In our own way."

"Very well," she finally agrees. "But any more shenanigans, and we're getting involved. I guarantee you won't like it."

I push to my feet. "I don't do shenanigans. Nobody under the age of forty does shenanigans."

"Where are you going?" she asks.

"I have homework." I walk to my room and don't breathe until the door shuts behind me. I'm not crying this time. I just want to sleep. So I shove my air pods in my ears, turn on some music, and sink into the comfort of my pillow.

Two hours later my mom whoops in the other room and wakes me up—she was probably in the middle of her evening spin routine. My hand reaches for my phone on the nightstand, then I remember there's nothing there I really want to look at. God only knows what texts I've gotten. The whole school is having one hell of a time rehashing all of this.

I have to look. Nine texts and one missed call.

I don't recognize the number but they left a voicemail.

Jack.

He only gets fifteen minutes of phone time per week. Why is he calling me?

The notification pops up for a voicemail, and I play it.

Hey Blue, it's me. Um . . . just wanted to say hi. Mom says you might need somebody to talk to. But . . . um . . . I guess you're busy. So . . . um . . . later, Barfinator.

There's a twinge of pain at the use of his familiar sign-off—a reference to the time I was seven and threw up on a carnival ride.

He sounds normal. Like he isn't where he is. My nostalgia doesn't last long as a wave of fresh anger sweeps over me. Mom says I need talking to? Did she tell him what happened today?

She is completely delusional if she thinks talking to Jack will make any of this better. He started this whole mess, and Maya is the one who won't let it go. I don't need to be talked to. I just need everybody to leave me the hell alone.

I toss the phone to the floor with a groan and roll my face back into my pillow.

THE ONLY THING worse than serving five days of suspension is serving five days in a house with my mother. At first, she made me get all my homework done, but when that only killed half of the first day, she demanded that I watch a documentary on Netflix and write a report about it for extra credit in Poly Sci. That got us to mid-afternoon. After that, she had me stuffing plastic bags full of brochures, coupons and product samples for her. She called it a *mini internship*. I call it hell.

Day two, I was left alone since she had to make product deliveries and go to lunch with a group of women in her direct line—the one that goes straight down the pyramid of stupid expensive products. Anyway, it's an excuse for her to go to lunch with a bunch of women and drink wine and bitch about their difficult suburban lives. I'm just grateful that my mini internship didn't extend to attending that lunch, so I was left blissfully alone for the rest of the day.

Day three was pure misery as Mom demanded I make up a spreadsheet with all my potential college choices and their admission requirements. When I told her there was plenty of time for that, I got an extended rant about the trajectory of my life and the importance of staying on track—which was all kinds of entertaining.

Day four put her into deep-cleaning mode. I was ordered to go through my closets and dressers, removing items for donation to the local Goodwill store. That only took up the morning, so after lunch she handed me a bucket full of cleaning products and told me to clean bathrooms and if I still had time to kill, I was supposed to sweep and mop the kitchen floor. I reminded her that we have a cleaning lady and she reminded me that it's Thursday and the cleaning lady doesn't come again until Monday. Then she launched into the *you need to learn what an honest day's work is like* speech—as if I didn't already work a crap job. I shut myself in the bathroom and played on my phone and never mopped the kitchen.

Today is my final day of this idiocy and she's got a mani-pedi and a haircut, then a sales strategy meeting with her 'top motivators,' followed by a home party this evening. I get to chill out for a good, long time.

I have to say I'm kind of liking the laying on the couch and watching Netflix aspect of a five-day suspension, but I also wonder if this is going to show somewhere when it comes time for my college applications to go in. I've never been suspended before. Is it an addendum onto your transcript? Do college admission counselors call and talk to your high school counselor to get the real deal on you?

My logical mind tells me that's probably not how it is, but if you ask either of my parents, it is absolute Armageddon and I have officially thrown my life away. I'm going to end up in a gutter with a needle in my arm after a hard night's work of prostitution, begging passers-by for their pocket change all because I was clumsy enough to fall into someone.

My stomach clenches as I wallow in the misery of it all. What good is a five-day suspension anyway? I still have to do all my homework while I put up with my mother. I guess that's the point. It's supposed to feel like hell on earth.

Mom actually asked me last night if I want to maybe do a cyber-school. Because being home with her every single day packing boxes full of leggings and protein shakes is exactly what I want to be doing in between bouts of homework. I'd rather eat broken glass.

My phone lights up and it's Jules.

"You know you're livin' the life?" She asks after I answer.

"You know it. Netflix and snack food," I reply.

"At least Maya got suspended too."

"She should have gotten longer. She started it."

"Yeah, but you sent her to the emergency room."

"Oh please," I say. "I don't even think she's hurt."

"Word around school is you guys were beating on each other with your fists and now Maya might need surgery on her foot," she tells me. "They're saying that you were trying to crush any hope she has of a college basketball scholarship."

"*What?*"

"Somebody even said you punched Ramsey in the face."

"Seriously? Oh my God!"

"They're saying that new guy—"

"His name is Devon," I interject.

"I know, I know. Everyone is saying he's skipping school to be with you. Is he there?"

"No, he isn't here. He's skipping school?"

"Nobody's seen him all week." Jules points out. "You in at four or five tonight?"

"Neither one," I say in a disgusted tone. "Mom says if I can't go to school, I can't go to work this week, either."

"Hank's going to have a cow."

"He already had one, ground it up, fried it on the grill, and shoved it down my throat," I grumble. "I'll be lucky if I have a job when this is over."

"You can always sell those stupid aromatherapy necklaces in your upstairs closet," Jules adds helpfully. "Doesn't your mom still have like, sixty boxes of them?"

"That's an idea," I tell her. "If I end up having to live on the streets, at least I have an income stream. Any other news?"

"That guy Josh is trying to talk to Allie B about prom." Jules is now eating something. I can hear her mouth slurping and crunching.

"It's not even February," I point out.

"I know, right?"

"And Allie is a lesbian," I add, a fact everybody in school is aware of.

"She told him that," Jules says. "He keeps telling her she just hasn't met the right guy."

We say those last five words in unison.

"Men." I say.

"So you're back on Monday?" Jules asks around another mouthful of whatever.

"I think I could be truly happy sitting in pajama pants on a couch for the next year-and-a-half. We just need to find some-place else for my mother to live." I answer.

"You're not getting rid of me that easy," Jules says. "It's boring here without you."

"I'm bored, too," I say. "It's like peak pandemic days all over again. Only without the paranoia."

"If you had another week, your mom would come up with something. Remember how she was?"

I shudder at the memory of essential oils in diffusers all over the house, of forty flavors of hand sanitizer clipped to purses and shoved in pockets, and the daily handful of vitamin supplements she forced us all to choke down, thinking it would bolster our immune systems.

"Please don't remind me," I beg. "I used to throw all those vitamins in that shoe box under my bed."

"Right next to the french fry stash."

Jack used to sneak in chicken nuggets and burgers from his after-dinner junk food raids. Mom thought he was out running. He kept me stocked with french fries and I helped him by writing a couple of essays for him.

"Fun times," I say in a flat voice. But I'm smiling at the memory.

"I gotta go pee before fourth block," she says unceremoniously. "Later."

"Later," I repeat. I end the call and look at the time. What to do with the rest of my day? Despite what I told Jules, Netflix is losing its charm.

I grab my coat and fish my car keys out of my pocket. Ugh. If I drive anywhere, Mom's going to accuse me of going to the mall or something. I leave the car keys on the counter and go for a walk instead, which is a healthy step to a *radiant new me*, so she can't complain if she comes home early for some bizarre reason.

The playground is deserted, of course. I don't know why I came over here. I guess I thought if Devon was skipping school maybe this was where he would be. But who lives their life at a playground? Me and him, but not today.

I'm going to walk around the neighborhood. Mom can't give me too much grief over physical activity out in the sun, soaking up the Vitamin D that I didn't get because of my refusal to drink a metaphysical mango shake this morning.

I find Willow Court, but have no idea which house. His car should be easy enough to find if I walk around the cul-de-sac. Maybe his last name is on the mailbox and I can leave him a note if he isn't there. Or not. That sounds stupid. Besides, I'd have to go home and get paper.

No car, no last name on the mailbox. I finish my tour of the street and head for home, deciding to walk the long way back by the playground again—partly because I'm kind-of looking for Devon but mostly because I really don't want to go home yet.

I'm just about to turn the corner when a familiar powder blue Volkswagen Bug pulls up next to me.

"You ditching school?" Devon asks through the open window.

"No. Are you? They tell me you weren't at school today. Or all week."

"Oh they do, do they? You really shouldn't be getting your news from *They*. Why weren't you at school?"

"I'm suspended. How don't you know that?"

"Hop in," is all he says.

"Where are we going?"

"Does it matter?"

I checked the time on my phone. Mom has that home party to attend tonight—something about making customizable charm bracelets with empowering catchwords on artisanal clay beads. She won't be back until at least nine or maybe even ten if they're serving wine. Dad is on a business trip and won't be home until the middle of next week. And I am sick of sitting around watching TV.

I open the door and slide into the seat next to him. "Any ideas?" I ask as I fasten my seat belt.

"Well," he says thoughtfully, as if chewing the idea over in his mind. "You've been suspended and I've been out all week shoveling a steaming load of my own life. I think we can both use a break."

"Is everything okay?"

He shrugs. "I'm dealing."

I want to ask him what in his life is keeping him out of school, but I get the feeling he would have told me more if he wanted me to know.

"You're not going to ask me about the suspension?" I give him a look of mild surprise. I'm not one to pry, but he is.

"When we're talking about you and Maya, any idiot can know that putting the two of you in a room after school and making you talk to each other is going to end badly. At least right now."

I slump down into the seat. "Tell that to Mrs. Ramsey."

"Nope. She has to slog through it for herself."

He puts the car in gear and I glance across at him, remembering how he looked that day on the playground. His hand is out of the bandage now, but he still has scabs and bruises on his knuckles. His face looks drawn, and there are shadows under his eyes.

He's a mystery and I don't know him well enough to know if that's a good thing or a bad thing. Today, I'm going to figure that out. I'm tired of talking about me.

"THE MOVIES? REALLY?" I raise my brows as Devon pulls into a parking space in front of the movie theater.

"Don't you like movies?"

"I like them fine. But in the middle of the day? On a weekday?"

"I didn't realize there was a social rule about appropriate times for movie viewing," he says with a shrug. "I guess things are done differently in Pennsylvania than in the rest of the world."

"It's fine," I say. "I just don't go to movies in the middle of the day on a weekday."

"Because you're in school," he reminds me.

"Because I'm in school."

"So this will be a whole new experience for you." He rubs his hands together with over-exaggerated glee. "How exciting!"

"It's not a new experience for you?"

He waves me off. "Nah. Been there done that, bought the popcorn. It's a great little getaway."

"You've spent the whole week going to movies?"

"Of course not. I also started online guitar lessons, went sledding for the first time on that hill behind the playground—hella fun— and I learned how to bake my own pita bread from a gif tutorial."

"You did all that?"

"Yeah."

"This week?"

"Yeah. Come on."

What the hell, I'm still watching movies but at least I'm off the couch. "So what are we seeing?" I ask.

He holds the door open for me as we walk into the foyer and then he points up at the marquee behind the box office worker in the booth.

"Take your pick," he says. "Doesn't really matter."

I give him a mildly annoyed look. "There's nothing really good out right now."

"Don't I know it," he says. "When every choice is a bad choice then *one* of them must be better, comparatively speaking."

"Don't try to share pearls of wisdom," I advise. "You're really not good at it."

"Noted."

I shake my head as I peruse the titles. "*Slash and Burn* doesn't look too bad," I say.

"Hmmm. What's your backup?"

"*Her Majesty's Assassin* might be interesting. That's a spy movie with that chick from the superhero thing."

"Sounds vaguely appealing," Devon nods sagely and my face cracks into a grin. "Let's do it.'

He pulls a wallet out and steps forward before I can reach into my coat pocket for my own wallet.

"You don't have to—"

He waves his hand as if to tell me it's no big deal. The girl in the ticket booth barely even looks up at him. Devon scoops up the tickets and holds the door into the concessions lobby for me.

"I can get the popcorn since you got the tickets," I tell him.

"Damn right you'll get the popcorn," he replies. "It's a lot more expensive than a couple of tickets. I'm going to want Milk Duds, too. You look like a Junior Mints kind of girl."

I shake my head. "Sour Patch Kids."

He points off toward a stand of candy at the far register. "They're down there. Want to share a soda? They're like a half gallon here."

"I only drink diet," I warn.

"Why?" He gives me a look up and down.

"Because all that sugar is bad for you."

"So are all those chemicals," he says. "That's what diet soda is—a cup of chemicals."

"You want water instead?"

"I'm thinking . . . slushy."

"Sugar." I remind him.

He puts his hands on his hips, exasperated. "I thought we were living a little today."

He's right. I sound like my mother. "Can we get cherry?"

"I knew we'd get along," he says, smiling wide. "Cherry is vastly superior to Blue Raspberry."

"It's not even a natural flavor. There are no blue raspberries."

"Unnatural." He gives a mock shudder. "An abomination of a flavor."

"It should be punishable by law." I grin. I'm loving the banter.

I head down toward the other register to get my candy and as I'm walking back I realize he's already ordered the popcorn and slushy and he's telling the girl at the counter to add in my Sour Patch Kids and his Milk Duds.

I push up next to him and pull out my wallet. His hand comes over and pushes my wallet away. I put my hand on top of his to remove it from my wallet.

"I've got this, remember?" I tell him.

"I invited *you*, remember?"

"If we fight about this I will win," I tell him. "And I *will* make a scene."

He takes a step back, raising his hands in a gesture of peace. "All right, all right, you've got this one."

We scoop up the popcorn and slushy, pocket our candy and make our way into the darkened interior of the theater. They haven't started the previews yet so the typical movie ads are blaring, begging us to download apps or sign up for rewards memberships. After a few moments our eyes adjust and it's clear that we are the only ones in the theater.

We pick seats right in the center and settle in. Devon shifts the popcorn over so that I can reach into it.

"So . . . what were you doing out and about in the neighborhood?" he asks

"I was just looking for something to do this afternoon."

"You were looking for me."

"I was walking."

"You were walking around the neighborhood looking for me. Or do you always take a stroll around my cul-de-sac?"

"It's a big neighborhood. I can walk wherever I want to walk."

"You didn't answer my question."

I make a face. "Okay, I was looking for you but only because Jules told me you haven't been in school all week."

"Hmmmm," is all he says.

I still remember how he looked on the playground the other night and I haven't asked him a thing about it or about himself. I feel small and petty and selfish. He's listened to me day after day and I've used him shamelessly as a sounding board without giving him a chance to do the same.

"Do you—do you want to talk about it?"

He stares ahead and reaches for the popcorn again, shoving some in his mouth and chewing thoughtfully.

"I'm not sure how much to tell you."

"It's okay," I say carefully. "I mean, it's probably hard moving to a new place right in the middle of the school year. You must miss your friends a lot."

"Yeah, I miss them."

"And you probably had a girlfriend there, right?"

The corner of his mouth quirks up. "Like, somebody I would take to the movies? In the middle of the day? On a weekday?"

He caught me and I fumble to recover. "I—I didn't mean—"

"Sure you did. And no, I didn't leave a girl behind. I can't imagine you'd go out with me next time if I told you I had a girlfriend in Florida."

"Next time?"

"Do you think I'm going to leave it at one date?"

"So this is a date?"

"You don't think it's a date?" He's still playful, but his eyes are wary.

"I like to be asked first."

"I did ask. And you said yes and got in the car and here we are."

"Here we are."

"We've got six minutes until the movie starts," he says. "That'll give you time to decide whether this is a date or not."

I give a nervous little laugh. "No pressure, right?"

He turns in his seat so he can face me more fully. "So you decided to come with me today—why, exactly?" He asks. "Are you completely against this being the start of something? Maybe something great for both of us?"

I stare at him like a deer in headlights.

"It's okay," he says, sitting back and taking a drink of slushy. "I didn't mean to put you on the spot. You don't have to give me an answer. Let's just enjoy the movie."

"I'm not trying to say I wouldn't date you," I tell him. "It's just—with everything going on at school and all—"

"I know what it's like to have a complicated life." He takes another long pull of the slushy. "Maybe a complicated life is easier when you've got somebody you can escape with."

I hold his gaze. "Maybe it is."

"I want you to know—aaaugh!" He suddenly grabs his head in both hands, crunching his palms into his temples as his eyes screw up tight.

"Devon! Are you okay?"

"Brain freeze," he grinds out, rocking back and forth in his chair.

I sock him on the shoulder. "Jerk! I thought you were going to tell me you had a brain tumor or something."

"I might have one after that," he says, rubbing gingerly at his temples. "That was a bad one."

He reaches for the slushy again and I shake my head as he takes another pull.

"The trick is—" He hands me the popcorn and sets his drink in the cup holder. Then he shoves both thumbs into his mouth and presses them up, behind his front teeth. "To warm up the roofth of your moufth."

I can barely understand him around his fingers.

"I'll just sip slowly, thanks."

He pulls his thumbs out, wiping them on his jeans. "I can see how this would not be sexy. Have I blown our first date already?"

I shift my eyes to the screen, a mysterious smile on my lips. "No."

He folds his hands across his chest with a satisfied smile. "Official first date: confirmed."

THE MOVIE WASN'T bad. It wasn't good, either, but I think it did what we both wanted it to do: it took our minds off our lives for a little while. Or maybe just being together did that. I'm willing to take a step back and consider that. We laughed all the way through the movie, mocking some of the more ridiculous plot convenience moments, mimicking a few choice bad lines. We even had a popcorn catching contest that progressively moved from sitting next to each other to throwing across the entire auditorium. It was hilarious and I haven't had that much fun in, God, I don't know how long.

The first half of the ride home is just a continuation of that vibe for a while. But then we have this silence—like we both realize we have to go back home, and back to what we were dealing with before we took this break. It occurs to me that he managed to push aside my earlier questions. I still don't know what's making his life as hard to live as mine is right now.

"So, are you going to tell me why you're at home?" I asked hesitantly. "Did you get suspended, too?"

His eyes don't leave the road as he drives, but he waves a dismissive hand. "Nah. I'm never in trouble. I stay firmly under the radar."

"So—mental health day?"

He shrugs. "Mental health day that turned into a mental health week. I'm excused, don't worry."

"Oh." I don't know what else to say to that. But I feel like I should say something. "I don't want you to think I'm sticking my nose into your personal life."

"Well, we *are* dating now." He turns his head to grin at me.

I smile back, and keep going. "But I know you're dealing with something. It's okay if you don't want to talk about it. But if you do want to talk, I'm here. I know I don't seem like a good listener—"

"I would never say that," he says emphatically. "You've got a lot going on. I get it."

"I just feel kind of bad," I tell him. "You've been listening to me for weeks now. And I know everybody's got their own stuff to deal with. You've been dealing with mine *and* yours, and I appreciate it."

"All part of my diabolical plan to get you to date me," Devon says, adding a maniacal cackle that makes me laugh out loud. "Now that we're dating, it all dries up. I'm cold and emotionless from now on, and it's going to be up to you to decide if I'm a manipulative villain, or if you're going to melt my frozen heart."

"I see," I nod slowly. "Then we'll just have to take it one day at a time."

"That's the best way to live a life."

Devon pulls up at the end of my block just in case any of my mom's nosy stay-at-home mom friends wanted to give her a report on my whereabouts. I start to reach for the door handle and then belatedly remember we were sort-of on a date.

"I had fun today," I say. And I did. I really did.

"I want a rematch on that popcorn contest. You barely beat me."

"I caught six more pieces of popcorn in my mouth than you did," I remind him.

"Yeah, but my throwing hand is still bruised. You had an advantage."

I bite my lip as if considering. "Fair enough. Next time you can move two steps closer."

"So there *is* going to be a next time?"

He makes it casual, leaning in with his elbow on the back of the seat. His eyes hold mine and for some reason, I'm not breathing evenly.

"Yes," I tell him. "Yes, I'd like that."

And then he moves forward slowly, and his lips brush my cheek. He must've read the disappointment in my eyes when he pulls back because he smiles slightly.

"I'm saving the real kiss for an officially-sanctioned date," he says.

"You told me this *was* a real date."

"It was, but more like a stealth date. A guerrilla date, if you will."

"Guerrilla date. I like that."

"I like it too," he says and then he reaches out with his finger and taps the end of my nose. "And I like you. So when I give you that first official kiss it's going to come with all the bells and whistles."

I raise a brow. "Balloon drop? Glitter? Pyrotechnics?"

He gives me a mocking half-bow "As my lady commands."

I started to reach for the door handle again, but his hand on my shoulder stops me.

"Since we're officially a *whatever* now," he says, "don't you think I should have your digits?"

"Oh, uh—yeah, of course." I dig out my phone, and impatiently swipe away a half-dozen notifications before I open it up to contacts and add his number in. I text him so he has mine.

"Hi?" He says, looking affronted as he reads my text. "That's hardly first text material."

"It's a guerrilla text," I say.

"Hmmph." He shoves his phone back down inside his coat pocket.

"Later," I say, finally opening the door.

"Any time after now is later," he reminds me. "I'll text you after dinner. Or maybe in five minutes."

I give him a smile, and the door shuts behind me. He makes a big show of looking straight forward as he drives past me, like he doesn't even know me, and I laugh.

I feel like I'm thirteen again and sneaking back into my house after meeting Jules under the plastic frog canopy on the playground where we'd watch all the YouTube videos my mom wouldn't let me watch.

Grabbing the mail out of the mailbox, I idly sort through it as I walk through the house. My mind replays my afternoon, and the warmth of his breath and lips on my cheek.

I have to admit, for a guerilla date it was pretty good.

He gets my humor. Most guys my age don't do humor well. They're too busy thinking about how much they want to get laid, or they're too busy obsessing about some other girl and they're half distracted when I'm trying to banter. Or they're like Austin, and if it doesn't involve a ball, a scoreboard, alcohol, weed, or something blowing up, it's pretty much not worth talking about.

Okay, not all guys. Not all the time. I'm overgeneralizing. But it does feel that way—a lot. Devon and I clicked. We just clicked. Every joke we made about the movie, every plot twist we saw coming, every time we hit each other in the face with popcorn trying to land a goal in each other's mouths—it was stupid, goofy fun. And I really needed some stupid, goofy fun.

In fact, the whole afternoon was great, and a great start as far as first dates go with the exception of one tiny little thing.

I still know next to nothing about him. I made an effort, I mean, a real effort to talk to him. To find out more about him and his life instead of everything always being about me. He did tell me a few things about his old school in Florida. He'd been on the golf team there and was a little disappointed we didn't have a golf team.

"A rich private school like Audubon?" He'd said, waving his hands in exasperation. "How is it that none of you golf? That's a no-brainer. I suppose nobody plays water polo either?"

"We do have high tea every Friday at three," I responded. "And don't you know? Golf is so early 2000's. Nobody who's anybody is golfing anymore."

He'd sniffed, and tilted his soda up to take a drink, making sure his pinky was properly extended. Then he deflected me into a conversation about *Fahrenheit 451*. We have a presentation due in a few weeks and neither of us have picked our book yet. We had a great time tossing titles off each other, everything from *Pride & Prejudice & Zombies* to various erotica titles we found on Amazon, with each suggestion growing more bizarre and hilarious. Before I knew it, the movie was over, we barely saw any of it, and I still didn't know much about him on a personal level.

But hey, it was only a first date, right? We've got time for that. Because there's going to be a second date. And life is finally going to be about something other than this situation with Maya and Jack.

I think I like that. I think I like that a lot.

"WELCOME BACK TO the both of you," Mrs. Ramsey says from her squeaky chair behind her desk. "I hope you've spent this week wisely and done a bit of self-reflection."

We both make non-committal noises, and neither of us bothers to elaborate. I see Maya's eyes drift to the clock on the wall and I'm right there with her. Let's just get this over with.

"Maya, I was very glad to hear that your foot is on the mend."

Maya's face changes at the remark. The boredom disappears, and she winces—just enough to tug some sympathy into Mrs. Ramsey's eyes.

"It's a little better," she says with a dramatic sigh. "I should be able to practice with the team tomorrow afternoon."

"Well, don't overdo," Mrs. Ramsey cautions.

Overdo her performance, I think. Drama queen. I'm surprised she didn't bring a pillow to prop her foot on.

"Today," Mrs. Ramsey says, "I thought we could talk a little about how the—event that you share has shaped your time here at Audubon. *Just* your time here at school," she qualifies, holding up one hand. "It might be beneficial to get a look at the other perspective."

"Doubtful," Maya mumbles.

"And I want to stress that this is not a contest," Mrs. Ramsey goes on. "We're not trying to keep score over who has it the worst in this situation. I think we can all agree Maya has a more significant loss and life-altering circumstance."

I can't argue with that. Part of me feels like I want to, though. Then I feel like an asshole for feeling like that. Hell, I don't know what I feel anymore except miserable.

"So let's just concentrate on how your shared event shapes your lives during the school day," Mrs. Ramsey says. "Maya—do you feel like people treat you differently since you've come back?"

"Well, yeah," Maya says incredulously. "I am the girl with the dead father."

"And you're also the girl who left school and recently returned," Mrs. Ramsey said. "In a way, that brought everything back to the forefront again. If you had remained in school, it's unlikely anyone would have been mentioning it this far down the road."

"Yeah. I guess." Maya shrugs. "But my Mom needed my help with our business trying to replace my Dad. It all took time to figure out and hire somebody in."

I hadn't considered that. At first I thought she just got bored at home, then I figured she did it so she could torment Jack through me. It never occurred to me she might have wanted to come back, and couldn't.

"And Blue," Mrs. Ramsey continues. "People are treating you differently with the advent of Maya coming back to school. That's fair to say, isn't it?"

"Yes." I want to keep going. I want to tell her that maybe this would've died down in a few days if Maya had kept her mouth shut and concentrated more on basketball than me. I mean, she's hurting herself as much as me by keeping all this drama churning. But I am determined to get through this session as peacefully as possible. If I have to sit through another kitchen table talk with my mother, I will drive myself off a cliff.

"Maya, can you expand a little on what it's like to come to school every day?" Mrs. Ramsey asks. "What sort of remarks have hurt or upset you? Will you share a little of that?"

Maya looks like she'd rather climb in the car next to me as I drive myself off that cliff. But she gives another half shrug and opens her mouth.

"I don't know. Just—people saying that Jack Mancini got away with murder. And that Blue is all full of herself about it."

"That's not true!" I snap. "And who the hell is saying my brother is a murderer?"

Maya raises her brows. "Everybody."

"Maya." Mrs. Ramsey's tone is a little sharper. "That's more than a bit of over-generalization. I walk these halls every day, too. I hear student conversations all day long. The entire school is not talking about this—or at least they hadn't been. The two of you have managed to build a perfect prison for yourselves with your behavior. We need to try to find a way to help you deconstruct that."

She leans back in her chair, steepling her fingers and looking at me over the tops of them. "Blue? Let's hear your side of this. What sort of things are being said that are hurtful to you?"

"You can pull up any one of her social media accounts," I say pointing at Maya. "Just read them. You want a list of every bad thing that's being said? It's all there."

"I'm not interested in your interactions with Maya at the moment," Mrs. Ramsey clarifies. "What are other students saying?"

"That I punched you in the face after I deliberately broke Maya's foot," I say waving my hand in the air. "That I broke my boyfriend's hand, too. That my brother killed a man and his plea bargain is somehow my fault, too, because my father makes a lot of money."

"Let's talk about that, then." Mrs. Ramsey leans forward. "So there is an assumption that because you have a certain level of privilege, it affected the outcome of the court trial."

"Obviously." Maya interjects.

Mrs. Ramsey holds up a finger to silence her. "That's for a judge or jury to decide. But that assumption of privilege is also affecting the perception of you here at Audubon, and in a very different way from Maya."

"I can't help it if my dad makes money," I protest. "A lot of people have parents that make good money. It's not my fault Maya doesn't fit into that group."

"And that's because I'm a scholarship student, right?"

"That wasn't what I meant."

"My parents were married for twenty-three years," she says, slapping her hand on the desk. "We own our own business. We've got a house in a nice neighborhood. We may not have your level of money but I'm not from some struggling, dirt-poor family. But none of that matters to you. All you see is another scholarship kid with Puerto Rican parents causing trouble in your rich little school."

"I never said that!"

Maya throws her hands up. "You didn't have to! I feel it! I feel it every day from every one of you and you have no concept of what that's like even for a minute. If I didn't play basketball, I would have no value here. I'm not rich enough or white enough and no matter how good my GPA is, no one thinks I'm smart enough."

I roll my eyes. "Projecting."

Mrs. Ramsey rests her chin in her palm, two fingers stretching up the side of her face.

"What makes you say that?"

I shrug, but it's stiff and tight. I suddenly feel like I'm under a microscope. "I just think she's exaggerating. Nobody's like that here. I've never heard anybody say that stuff."

Maya starts to interrupt, and Mrs. Ramsey holds up a hand to silence her.

"You have some decent friends, in that case," she says to me. "But a statement like 'nobody's like that here' draws completely from your own experience as a wealthy, healthy, heterosexual, young white woman in a wealthy, predominately white private school. Her experience is not your experience. Can you understand that, at least?"

"She can't," Maya grumbles. "Nobody ever treats her or her family like they don't belong."

"So give her an example," Mrs. Ramsey encourages. "When did you have to deal with someone treating you badly?"

"I've been called names. People have asked me if we live with all my grandparents and aunts and cousins in the same house. One of the teachers tried to give me a big bag of her daughter's clothes. She told me she knew I'd appreciate nice things."

"How about another time?" Mrs. Ramsey asks. "It doesn't have to be at school."

Maya does not want to talk about this anymore. She just shrugs, twirling a pencil in her fingers, back and forth.

"Last week," she finally says. "At work."

"In your family's coffee shop?"

Maya nods, still twirling the pencil. Her eyes tighten with the memory. "I was on my break, sitting at one of the tables. It was my Tia's birthday so I called her and we were talking in Spanish. Some lady came in and she tells me to speak English because I'm in America. I started to say something but my mom gave me this look like she'd kill me if I did, so I just went outside to finish talking. My mom told me after to just ignore that stuff because we need every customer. Like we have to put up with that shit for her five-dollar latte." She tosses the pencil down, then picks it back up and twirls some more. "Stuff like that."

Mrs. Ramsey leans forward. "So your mother was afraid to let you defend yourself?"

Maya shrugs. "She's always up in my face reminding me I have to always be better, do better, prove I'm as good as the rest of you." She sucks in a breath, pauses for a moment. Her voice gets softer. "My dad was different. He just let me be me."

My throat feels tight, and my eyes fill up. I blink hard a few times.

My mom is like that too, I think. But instead I say, "At least your dad was involved in your life."

"And that's supposed to make me grateful?" She snaps. "That I had a great dad while he was alive?"

Silence hangs between us and her words sting like a slap.

"I'm saying I don't have your kind of father." I don't know why this is coming out, but it is. It needs to come out. "I can count on one hand the number of family dinners I've had with my dad in the last year. He works all the time. He's got a pretty high level position at his company, and that's why we make lots of money. But it's kind of useless if you barely know each other. It's like we're all roommates. Not like we're family."

"At least you have a chance to tell him that," she says.

"I'll have to email his assistant and see if I can get on his calendar," I say bitterly. "And I'll have to get my mother to stop giving orders long enough to let me get a word in."

Maya just rolls her eyes, like I'm trying to make this a contest. It isn't a contest. I can't even begin to imagine what her life is like right now. My dad may be a distant figure, but he's still my dad. I love him. I wouldn't want to spend more time with him if I didn't love him. And if he were gone tomorrow? A shaft of pain hits me in the chest at just the thought. That would be a hundred, a thousand times worse if it was reality.

I don't have anything else to say. Nothing that would make a difference anyway. So I keep my mouth shut.

Mrs. Ramsey leans back in her chair and takes a deep breath in. "Well," she says. "We're making some actual headway here. And all of this just proves my point—it's easy to make assumptions about somebody when you don't really know them. And so far the only thing the two of you have in common is a really terrible thing that neither of you had any control over."

I want to nod but at the same time this isn't my terrible thing. I mean, it's been terrible for me but my piece of terrible is only a small percentage compared to what Maya has had to endure, on top of all the shit I didn't know she already had to deal with.

"I said it before, and I'll say it again," Mrs. Ramsey goes on. "I don't expect you two to be friends. But I think if we can find some common ground, maybe the two of you can learn to coexist without blood on the walls."

She pushes back from her desk and the wheels on her rolling chair squeak loudly. She rises to her feet. "I don't know about you girls, but I could really go for something to drink. I've got a six pack of Diet Coke in the teacher's lounge. And I think there are some leftover iced teas from last week's art show. I'll go get them if you promise to keep it civil while I'm gone."

I nod. Anything to break this up. At the very least it'll kill ten minutes. Maya must have the same idea because she nods too.

"Diet Coke is good," she says.

"I'll take one," I chime in.

Mrs. Ramsey smiles. "You see? You've got Diet Coke in common now."

I force myself to smile and Maya's forced smile is so bad I have to bite my lip to keep from laughing. She notices me noticing and bites her own lip as well. There's another thing we have in common. We both think this is bullshit.

The door closes behind Mrs. Ramsey and we sit in silence. I start tapping my pen on my notebook but it sounds ridiculously loud so I stop.

"How long before she asks us to move in together?" Maya makes a sound of disgust.

"Maybe she'll settle for us being prom dates," I deadpan. "I could put together a promposal."

Maya gives a snort. "That would only make her eyebrows arch even higher."

"Is that possible?"

"Seriously," Maya says. "Bitty has brows like a bug."

I huff out something like a laugh as the door opens and Mrs. Ramsey walks back in. We both stiffen. She notices, but doesn't say anything. I guess she's afraid to push it too much today. She hands us each a Diet Coke and then she sits behind her desk again, squeaking the wheels as she slides back in place.

"That chair is awful." I say.

"It is terrible," Mrs. Ramsey agrees. "I've tried putting WD-40 on it but it still squeaks. And there's no budget for new chairs. As always."

"Doesn't that bug you?" Maya asks, and I choke on my Diet Coke and begin to cough at her slight emphasis on the word *bug*.

"Are you all right?" Mrs. Ramsey asks.

"Yeah," I say in a strangled voice. "Just went down the wrong way."

"Okay, then," Mrs. Ramsey says. She takes a long pull on her Diet Coke, then sets it down. "I've been thinking about this ever since the two of you first came to my office. And as much fun as these afternoon sessions have been—" she turns her eyes to Maya and then to me. "I think we've finally reached a place where we can start working together toward a common goal."

Oh my God. She really does want us to move in together.

"Like what?" Maya asks warily.

"I'm thinking *club*," Mrs. Ramsey says.

I wrinkle my brow in confusion. "You want us both to join a club?"

"No, I want you both to *start* a club." She says. "Figure out something you both have an interest in that isn't already in existence here at Audubon. You can meet as little as every other week, if that's what works between part-time jobs and the basketball team. But come up with something together. Something productive. Something that has you both moving forward."

"So just pick a subject?" Maya clarifies. "Like we could have a coffee club?"

Holy hell, I could start a club selling my mom's products. Maya and I could both make bank and my mother would be out-of-her-mind thrilled with it. And it would get us out of these *getting in touch with your feelings* sessions. Sign me up.

"I think I can do that," I say looking over at Maya.

She gives a short little nod. "Twice a month? I could make that work."

"It's not going to be as quick and easy as you think," Mrs. Ramsey says. "At our next session I want you each to give me five options and the reasons you have for picking each one. Then we'll have a discussion and narrow it down to three between all ten suggestions."

"Easy enough," I say.

"I'm not finished," Mrs. Ramsey says. "Then I want you to research the top three so I know you're serious about this and you have a solid grasp of the subject you're trying to address.

We'll meet again to discuss our findings and from there we can move toward deciding on one."

"So we have to write essays, or something?" Maya asks, clearly irritated. I'm right there with her. We've got enough to do. This is starting to sound like more school after school.

"Nothing that formal," she reassures us. "Just take some good notes and be prepared to defend your points and share your information. Then I want to decide on governance. How are you going to set up your officers? Will you need fundraising? What sort of activities will you schedule that demonstrate your club principles? Is there a larger organization your club can affiliate with? That sort of thing."

I wonder how long we have to keep the club going. Probably only to the end of the school year. Clubs start over in the fall, and with both of us heading into our senior year, I'm sure we won't get any grief if we decide not to renew the club. After all, we're only doing this to make them happy and they know it. Like Mrs. Ramsey said, they don't expect us to be friends. This will just prove we can be civil around each other.

"You'll need to think about marketing it to the rest of the student population in order to get their interest," Mrs. Ramsey adds.

"I'm sure we can generate some buzz," I tell her, making sure I put a little emphasis on the word *buzz*. Now it's Maya's turn to choke on her Diet Coke.

"Sorry," she says, shooting me a conspiratorial look as Mrs. Ramsey turns away to grab a tissue for her.

"It's settled then," Mrs. Ramsey says with a very self-satisfied smile. "The newest Audubon club is in your hands."

DEVON IS LEANED over the trunk of my car when I walk out to the parking lot. As I get closer, I can see he's sketching something in a notebook.

"It's a bunny," I exclaim as I look over his shoulder. "Wow! That's really good."

"There's a bunch of them living in the bushes over there." He gestures with his pen. "I call this guy Freckles. See the marks by his nose?"

"They look like claw marks," I say, studying the picture.

"They are. He's tough, but adorable."

"You're really talented. Is this what you want to do? Art?"

"Yeah, but more graphic art and design. I'd love to help develop games, eventually. Or maybe celebrity ice sculptures. Haven't narrowed it down yet."

Okay, that makes me smile. "How long have you been here?"

"Not long. I was going to start working on the outline for the presentation in Linza's class."

I groan. "That freaking presentation. I haven't even started yet."

"Have you picked your book?"

"No. I'm really a very shallow person. Books have way too much depth for me. Why can't I be allowed to memorize a BuzzFeed article for posterity?"

"I refuse to believe that you are a shallow person," he says. "Not my girlfriend."

I roll my eyes, but the smile tugs at my lips anyway. "Didn't you get enough of that word at lunchtime?"

"What?" He says, the picture of wide-eyed innocence. "I like that word."

"You've called me your girlfriend at least forty times today, and in front of as many people as you could." I remind him.

"Does it bother you?" He asks, and the smile fades slightly. "If it's making you uncomfortable—"

I wave a hand. "It's okay. A little weird, but it doesn't really bother me. We *are* dating, after all."

He grins sheepishly. "I'm happy about it. One of the few truly bright points in my life at the moment."

Something in the way he says that carries the weight of a little too much truth. He's still smiling broadly, so I let it go for now.

"So how'd it go?" He asks.

"Nobody got injured," I answer grimly.

"That's better."

"I guess you could say that. Mrs. Ramsey laid a club on us."

His eyes widen. "She hit you with a stick?"

Despite my mood, that makes me laugh. Devon always knows how to make me laugh.

"She wants us to *start* a club."

"A club about what?"

I shrug. "Not sure yet. She's letting us decide."

He rubs his chin thoughtfully. "That should be interesting."

"We'll see. Where's your car?"

"It's getting new brakes so I got dropped off today," he said. "I told my parents my girlfriend could bring me home."

I shake my head and open the door, gesturing for him to get in on the other side. He slides in next to me, dropping a kiss on my cheek.

"Thanks, girlfriend."

"I do have a name, you know. Even if it's a goofy name."

"I told you, I like your name. Blue like the sky. Do you know the origin of my last name? Guthrie?"

I turn the key in the ignition and pull us out of the parking lot. "Is this a genealogy lesson?" I ask. "Or do you have really cool skeletons in the ancestral closet that I get to hear about?"

"This is straight up word origin," he says. "Guthrie is an Old English word that means wind."

"So your ancestors spent too much time at the burger bar," I say.

"Likely—but this is about how our names go together. The wind and the sky. Like we belong to each other."

We've only barely started dating. Why did my chest tighten— in a good way—when he said that?

"And someday," he continues in a lofty tone. "You'll take your rightful place at my side in the great kingdom of Beefador, where burgers grow wild in the fields and the peasants are sturdy."

I laugh, and he keeps me laughing all the way until I pull up in front of his house.

"So this is you? The one with the blue shutters?" I ask.

"Yeah, my mom hates them," Devon answers. "As soon as my dad has the time they'll be some other color."

"Please tell me your mother doesn't sell diet shakes or skin care products."

"Nope. She's got enough going on. She's not interested in that stuff."

"Well, make sure she doesn't get on my mom's radar. She's hit everyone else up in the neighborhood. Your mom would be fresh meat."

"Speaking of—" he says, turning his head toward the middle-aged woman who is now standing in the doorway. She doesn't smile or wave. She just stares at Devon expectantly before she turns and walks back into the house. Something about the look on her face makes his whole body tense.

"I've got nothing to do right now," I say carefully. "And my mom's gone until dinner time. I could stay for a little while, if you'd like."

Devon's mouth tightens and I could swear his face pales slightly.

"You *do* have something to do," he reminds me. "You need to pick a book and start an outline for your presentation. And I really have to go. We'll hang out another time."

Well, this is awkward. I force a smile. "Okay. Um—right. I should go."

"Hey." His voice is low, husky. "I'm not trying to get rid of you. I'd love to spend the rest of the evening with you. Hell, I'd love to sneak into your room through a window and have another popcorn war until we're both exhausted and fall asleep in each other's arms. Today's just not good for that, and believe me, I'm more disappointed than you are."

After that pronouncement, I'm really not sure he is.

"It's all right," I say. "We'll pick another day."

"We'll have plenty of them," he promises. "You're my girl-friend, after all."

I smile at the word, and my eyes begin to drift closed as he leans in. His warm breath brushes my lips and I slowly move my hands up his arms toward his shoulders. He starts low, at my neck. I feel his nose, his breath grazing my skin as his mouth slowly drifts up, raising gooseflesh on my skin. Then he shifts, and once again, I get a soft peck on the cheek. He pulls back.

"What the—" I begin to protest, but he extends one finger and places it lightly against my lips.

"Anticipation," he says, in that low husky voice. "It's a hell of a drug."

Then he opens the door and slips out. "Later!" He calls back over his shoulder.

I don't know whether to punch the steering wheel or laugh out loud. As I pull away, I watch as Devon approach his door. It's like there's an invisible weight on his shoulders, forcing them to droop, weighing him down with every step as he gets closer.

That picture stays in my mind as I pull into my driveway, and niggles at me as I grab the mail from the mailbox. Part of me wants to call him, or text him, break through that sunny, joking demeanor of his and get down to what's eating him underneath. But if he wants me to know, he'll tell me. I'm his girlfriend. I can wait to learn his secrets.

I lay the mail down on the kitchen counter and as the letters fan out, I recognize the handwriting on one of them.

Jack. And it's addressed to me.

My heart gives a funny little jump, and at the same time, I fight back my irritation. I just had a great half hour laughing in my car. Half an hour of time where I didn't think about anything other than hanging out with my boyfriend. It was a blessed relief. And I was looking forward to having a few more hours in the quiet of the house with Mom still gone to chill out and just relax.

But Jack wrote me a letter. Why did Jack write me a letter? I guess I'm not going to know the answer until I open it up, so I do.

Blue, he wrote.

I know this is bizarre getting a letter on actual paper delivered by the mailman, but they don't allow any electronics here. And maybe that's the only way I can talk to my sister. Not ragging on you. Just calling it like I see it.

Not ragging on me. Right.

Mom mentioned that you're having a rough time with Maya Rodriguez. I just want to say I'm sorry that I made it hard for you. You know I never wanted that to happen. I wish it hadn't.

I wish that, too.

Eventually, everybody will get tired of talking about this and life will go back to normal for you. So at least one of us gets that.

What? Am I supposed to feel sorry for him?

And I know you don't want to hear what Mom and Dad are telling you, but they're right. Just ignore her. It takes two people to fight.
I'm speaking from personal experience when I tell you that if only one person wants to make contact, not a lot is going to happen.

Nice. Nice jab, Jack.

Things here are going okay. The instructors are actual drill sergeants retired from the military and they all have God complexes. They are determined to scare us straight. I'm here with a bunch of druggies and criminals and it's just really annoying more than anything. I'm bored a lot when they aren't running us into the dirt. They make us all do chores. I'm stuck in the laundry three hours a day and I haven't even told Mom that because she'd love it.

She *would* love it.

She did notice my chapped hands and gave me her twenty-dollar hand cream. They confiscated it, so I guess some drill sergeant is using it to moisturize his cracked elbows. Maybe I can work out a downline for her here. LOL.

I smile as I read that. She would totally go for that if he actually managed to do it.

I know you're busy with school and the job and everything, but it would be nice to see you one of these Sundays. No pressure.

I don't have any friends here, and none of my friends back at home visit. I think they're afraid for anyone to know they have contact with me. Like I've got a disease or something. Not that it matters, since I'm going to Boston in the fall. I guess you know who's got your back and who can't be bothered.

Okay, that one hurt.

So come and see me when you get a chance. I've got four more months in this place and no twenty-dollar hand cream to see me through.

Jack

P.S. I told somebody here about the Frito theory, and he agreed with us.

I hold the letter in my hand for a moment, just staring at his familiar scrawl, not really reading the words. There's an ache in my chest as my eyes begin to focus again and I can hear his voice clearly in my head as I read between the lines.

Eventually, everybody will get tired of talking about this and life will go back to normal for you. So at least one of us gets that.

Life will never go back to normal for any of us. My parents will always be the parents of that kid who killed a man and got off with a slap on the wrist. Sure, their friends would never be impolite enough to bring it up, but just like my friends, they're all probably thinking it. My parents know that. They carry on like none of it ever happened, like if nobody talks about it, it'll just go away. And I suppose it will to some degree. Eventually something juicier will happen to somebody else in their circle—an affair maybe, or a business going under. Their friends will all have something new to gossip about, but it'll never be totally forgotten. Not by them and not by us.

A year and a half from now, I'll be graduating and going away to college. If I'm lucky, I'll pick a college nobody from my school is attending and maybe nobody there will know or even care that any of this happened to my brother. A logical part of my brain knows that even here at Audubon, the whole school can't talk about this forever. It's already starting to fade a bit on the edges. Not fast enough for me of course, but it's fading all the same.

But life will never go back to normal for Jack. He might sound like he's making jokes and just keeping his head down and getting through this, and that his life would just continue in forward motion when he goes to college and he's away from here. But he lived that night. He lived it firsthand. He felt his car swerve, heard the squeal of the tires, and watched in horror as the other car tumbled down the incline. He made the call to 911 on his cell phone, knowing full well that he might be over the limit when the EMTs and the cops arrived. He still made the call anyway.

And then he sat there by the car, watching as they used the Jaws of Life to pry the door apart and pull Maya's father from the wreckage. Jack watched as they worked on her dad right there on the side of the road and continued to work on him as they loaded him into the ambulance.

I was with my brother at the hospital when the doctor came in and told us that Maya's father had died. I had no idea he was her father at the time—none of us did. We didn't even know his name. They told us the dead man had a wife and three kids. I watched Jack's face as they told him that. I watched it crumple, watched as his hands came up, pressing hard into his eyes. Watched his shoulders shake.

Then my dad put a hand on Jack's head, telling him softly that it was all going to be okay. They'd called the lawyer, and it was all going to be okay.

I was sitting on a chair next to the hospital bed—they were keeping Jack overnight for observation since he had a concussion. I reached across and put my hand on his leg, just to let him know I was there. I was there for him. He dropped his hands, closed his eyes, and then reached down, sliding his fingers over mine.

My mother put her arms around him and told him the important thing was he wasn't badly hurt.

I remember thinking, *No, the important thing is somebody's dead. We're just grateful it isn't someone we love.*

"TED TALKS?" MAYA looks at me like I grew a second nose. "What, we're going to get up a couple of times a month and give a speech?"

"I was thinking we could get a group of people together and we could all pick something we're good at and give a talk about it. That's all." I try not to snap at her, but it's not like she's had any great ideas. Recycling club? How the hell do we turn that into an afternoon activity?

"You could give a talk about basketball," I suggest. "Everybody does a different topic every meeting and maybe we could post the talks somewhere."

"It's an interesting idea." Mrs. Ramsey taps her chin thoughtfully. "But it's also one that's going to need a lot of outside collaborators. First of all, you'll have to reach out to the AV club and get someone who can run the video camera and record so that you have a quality product—we'll want to put it on the school district website. Second, you'll need a teacher sponsor who's willing to review every video for content—and then that review will have to be repeated by either the principal or the vice principal to be sure nothing slips through that shouldn't be there. We don't want a TED talk about how to roll a joint or something coded in meme-talk that conveys hidden messages— things that might be outside the school's code of conduct or have sexual overtones."

"I didn't even think about that," I grumble.

"And then we have to figure out who's going to pick the topic each session," Maya says. "That's bound to piss somebody off."

I roll my eyes. "Do you have a better idea? Besides rooting through the dumpsters to make sure nobody tossed a cardboard box or a can of Coke in there?"

"That's not what I said," she protests. "This is going to take a month if you don't decide on something soon."

"Me? You're the one who turned up your nose at my pet collection idea. Who hates pets so much they won't collect food for them to donate to shelters and food banks?"

"I don't hate pets," she fires back. "I just don't think anybody's going to be lugging a twenty-pound sack of dog food on a bus into school with them."

"Which is a fair point," Mrs. Ramsey agrees. "Maybe you could set up cash donations and go out and buy the food yourself, find a way to deliver it. We'll come back to that one. Maya? What's your next idea?"

"We could do a book club."

Dammit. That one was on my list. Not that I want to do it, but I had to come up with something. Does her choosing it cancel it out of my list? One way to find out.

"I've got that on my list too, Mrs. Ramsey," I say.

She breaks into an instant smile. "Well, that's terrific! Something you both want to do. We may have this solved sooner than we thought."

I look over at Maya and she seems as enthused about it as I am. I bet she ran out of ideas, too.

"We could ask Mrs. Cobb in the library for recommendations," I offer.

"I think we should ask other students," Maya says. "She's only going to recommend award-winning books about stuff like bullying and history."

"That doesn't mean they're bad books," I retort. "Award-winning books win awards for a reason."

"Yeah," she says. "Because some room full of teachers and librarians decided they should."

"Perhaps you could do a mix of both," Mrs. Ramsey suggests. "Get input from the library reading list and from club members. Then you'll need to find a teacher sponsor—start with Mrs. Cobb—draw up a list of books for review, and come up with discussion questions for each book to submit to your sponsor ahead of time—"

"We can't just sort of talk about it?" I say. This is sounding more and more like homework. Discussion questions? I'll be lucky if I read the damn book.

"We could alternate meetings," Maya says. "I'll do the questions one time, and she can do the questions the next."

"Uh-uh," Mrs. Ramsey says, shaking her head. "Collaboration, remember? You two are working on this together—all the way through. You need to come up with your discussion questions together for every meeting. You need to run the club meeting together. And then at the end of every meeting, I'll expect a recap of what the participants liked and disliked about each book. We can publish that on the district website, on the library page."

Digging through a dumpster is starting to sound more appealing. Maya must agree, since she turns to me and says:

"What else have you got?"

"Umm . . . I was thinking maybe a spa club? Like, we meet and try out skincare products like facemasks or lotions, or give each other manicures. Just for fun."

Maya raises her eyebrows and makes a rude sound. "Spa Club. That is so completely you."

I tense up because she's putting me in that Rich Girl box again. And I can totally see how it would sound that way, but dammit, I'm trying to find something easy that we don't really have to do much for. She could work with me, here.

"It would have educational aspects," I say in my defense. "We can talk about stress relief techniques and self-care. We could call it the 'Audubon Oasis' or something like that. Maybe even introduce yoga or journaling."

"So we're not just talking about makeovers," Mrs. Ramsey says. "But you do have to decide how you're going to handle the product sampling. Is everyone expected to bring their own? Are you going to reach out to local retailers and try to get samples? Are people going to be sharing products? Because that's a hygiene concern. Maybe we'd be better off sticking with self-care and stress remediation. But you'll have to come up with a lesson plan every meeting."

I throw my pen down. "Every single idea comes with a ton of work."

"Seriously." Maya's tone echoes mine.

"Did I say this was going to be all fun and games?" Mrs. Ramsey asks. "I want you to find something you're both in agreement about—something that matters to both of you. If you find something you're both passionate about, it won't feel like work."

"It's just that I've got so much going on—"

Mrs. Ramsey interrupts me before I can go into it. "We've all got better places to be," she says tartly. "But the two of you got yourself into this and you're going to have to work to get through it."

"Well, we're getting nowhere today," Maya says. "Can we just go?"

I look up at the clock and we still have twenty-five minutes left. I'd rather get this solved today than have to come back and spin our wheels over it for another hour.

"Let's just get it over with," I say with a sigh.

"Some of us have lives," Maya snaps. "And they'd like to spend them with their remaining family members."

My eyes go wide. "Hey!"

"Maya!" Mrs. Ramsey says. "We are discussing club options at the moment. Let's not re-open old wounds."

Maya crosses her arms and slides down in her chair. "Just because she's not throwing me around doesn't mean we're buddies now."

"I never said we were," I growl back at her.

Mrs. Ramsey leans back in her chair, rubbing her temples with her fingers. "Okay—I think we need to take this in another direction. I want both of you to spend the next ten minutes writing down a list of hobbies and interests. Let's start there."

Maya groans and the word *ugh* spills out of my lips before I can help it. Mrs. Ramsey pushes back from the desk in her squeaky chair. "But first, since you're both wearing sneakers today and judging by last weekend's game, Maya's foot is fully healed—go take a run."

"Huh?" I look at her like she's nuts because she is.

"You heard me. Get some blood flowing to those beautiful brains of yours, and run off some of that aggression. Out the front door, lap the parking lot, and then come back."

There's no point in arguing, so I grab my coat and follow Maya out the door. Mrs. Ramsey stands at the doorway—I guess to make sure we're actually doing it. The parking lot is huge and L-shaped, and once we both get around the bend, we slow down.

Maya stops and I wonder if her foot is hurting her. I'm sure she was mostly faking—she's walking fine and playing basketball—so maybe she's thinking to milk it again. Still, I feel like I should say something.

"Are you okay?"

She gives me an annoyed look. "Yeah, and I'm not stupid. If we walk across we can cut off half of this stupid run. She can't see us anymore."

I look back over my shoulder. "You're right. Hell if I'm going to work up a sweat for her."

"Why can't she just let us go home?"

"We might as well get this finished. And by the way, I came up with spa club because I thought it would be easy. Neither one of us wants to do this, so let's pick something that won't take a lot of work."

Maya leans back against a car. "She's going to make it a lot of work no matter what we choose. And I really need to get out of here today. I have a birthday party to plan and I don't even know where to begin." She makes a disgusted sound and shoves her hair back off her face.

"For Haylee?" I ask. I know it's not Austin's birthday.

"My sisters," she says. "They're nine and twelve and their birthdays are two days apart. I haven't even started to plan." She pushes off the car, and starts walking across the lot.

"Hasn't your mom got any ideas?"

She whirls on me, and I realize instantly it was the wrong thing to say.

"No, she doesn't," she says scathingly. "My mom spends most of her days working at my family's shop, and the rest of the time she's too depressed to get out of bed. Planning a party for two kids after you've buried their father is not even remotely on her agenda."

I stare at her, stunned.

"I'm sorry," I finally say. "Seriously, I am."

I know life is hard for her since she lost her dad. Of course it is. I guess I just didn't think about all of the fallout. That's got to be hard for her little sisters, too. And now she has to step in and shoulder all of that.

She waves me off with her hand like she doesn't have time for me and she keeps walking.

"I can help." The words tumble out of my mouth, and the guilt dripping off of them instantly straightens her spine. She turns back to look at me again.

"I don't need your pity."

"It's not pity. I mean it. I can help you. I *want* to help you."

She crosses her arms and looks at me. "What? You're going to bake a cake?"

"No—I—what if you do Spa Club for their birthday? Like, give them makeovers, pass out some gift bags with skincare and nail care products, stuff like that?"

She looks taken aback but then her eyes shift as she considers. "They have six friends they're inviting over. I might be able to make that work. Maybe hit up the dollar store for some cheap face masks and makeup."

"Haylee could probably help you out, giving manicures and teaching them how to do their hair and stuff."

"Yeah, I guess."

"And—I can get you stuff, too." The seed of a wild idea is growing in my brain, and the more it grows, the more I really, really like it.

"What kind of stuff?" She asks, and then she shakes her head. "We don't need your cast-offs."

"No, this is fresh product. I've got all kinds of stuff. My mom reps a dozen different product lines, and there's always tons of leftovers. Clearance items. She has bins and bins full of stuff in our garage, in our closets. Usually she hands it out as giveaways for home parties, or as hostess gifts. She doesn't even know what she's got in there. I can go through it all and put together some gift bags for you to hand out."

The distrust is evident on her face. "Why would you help me?"

"Because I want your sisters to have a good birthday," I say. "And—" I pause, not sure how to say it so I just do. "And it's not fair you have to do everything."

"I told you, I don't want your pity."

"I don't pity you." That's not entirely true, and the look on her face says she knows it. But I really can help her, and I want to help her. If I can use a small amount of my mother's ridiculous stockpile of junk, I'm even happier to do it.

"I can pay you for it," she says. "We're not poor."

"I didn't say you were," I reply. "And I'm not trying to sweep in here like some privileged benefactor trying to show what a good person I am for donating some fancy products," I tell her. "We have the stuff. It's going to waste. And I'd rather know a group of little girls screamed and squealed and love the hell out of it then see it shoved in the tote bag of another forty-year-old woman sipping a glass of wine."

"This isn't going to buy my friendship," she says flatly.

"Look," I say. "We're *not* friends. I'm not trying to change that. But right now, I can help you. So let me."

"Okay," she finally says, blowing out a breath. "Okay. The party is Saturday, at two."

"Tomorrow's Friday. I work from six to close. Have Austin bring you by, and I'll have the stuff with me."

We both jump a little as we hear Mrs. Ramsey calling out our names.

"We'd better get back inside," I say. "She probably thinks we're punching each other or something."

"It'd almost be worth waiting to see if she comes running," Maya says. "See how she likes working up a sweat."

We take off in a slow jog and Mrs. Ramsey gives a wave as we come into view.

"I'll have Haylee bring me by," Maya says as we turn up the sidewalk. "Austin and I aren't together anymore."

"Oh?" I really don't know what else to say.

"Yeah. He's kind of boring. All he talks about is sports. Are you with that Devon guy?"

"Yeah."

"So he's feeling better?" She asks. "I saw him at the emergency room the night I went for my foot."

I stop, and then force myself to keep walking. "Really? I didn't know that."

Devon was at the emergency room? That would've been right before I was suspended. He didn't tell me he was sick. He looked fine when I saw him.

"He looked pretty bad," she tells me. "He was there with his parents and they brought him in an ambulance. Haylee said he was out the next week, when we were off."

"He was. He's better now."

"That's good. He seems okay. If you like that type." She gives a shrug. "Come on, let's get this over with."

I follow behind her, but my mind is whirling. What could have sent Devon to the hospital? In an ambulance? And why hadn't he said a word about it? I mean, I know I haven't been his girlfriend for long, but this is ridiculous. The guy doesn't want to talk about anything. A trickle of unease runs down my spine.

What isn't he telling me?

"DUDE, START A baking club. I'll join if I can get free food. Or maybe a taco club. Like, a different kind of taco every meeting. You could meet on Tuesdays."

Jules punctuates her suggestion by shoving a large handful of chips in her mouth, some of which fall out and scatter across my bed.

"Then we'd have to spend time waiting for stuff to cook," I say. "Plus, we'd have to clean up. And knowing Ramsey, we'll have to write up every recipe, pull the AV club in to produce a video of it, and then publish a cookbook at the end of the semester. But only after the vice principal has reviewed each recipe to make sure there isn't a secret sexual message inside."

"You could get pretty steamy with that," Jules says.

"Bananas and whipped cream."

"You could bake bread and do a whole series on shaped buns."

"We could bake gingerbread voodoo dolls, decorate them to look like teachers, and sell them at lunch."

Jules crams in another handful of chips. "Mmmff," she says, nodding in agreement.

"Just a thought."

"So what time is super-secretive skater boi coming by?" She asks, after she clears her mouth.

"He should be here any time. And his name is Devon."

She waves a chip-filled hand. "I know, I know. He seriously hasn't kissed you yet? Maybe he's waiting for Valentine's Day. Or his big secret is that he's gay."

"You don't go to the hospital in an ambulance just because you're gay." I point out.

"Maybe somebody beat him up."

"Don't you think that would've made the news? I'm sure his parents would've pressed charges. And I don't think he's gay. He's just—" I don't even know how to describe it other than to say that he's just Devon. I can't deny that it is odd that we haven't had our first kiss.

"We haven't been together that long," I remind her.

"Just sayin.' Maybe his parents found out and they're the reason he needed an ambulance. Have you met them yet?"

"No!" I deny vehemently. "I mean, no, I haven't met them but also no, his parents didn't beat him. He would mention if his parents were horrible people."

Something cold and awful twists in my stomach as I remember the way his mother looked that day when I dropped him off at the house. And that night at the playground—he was crying. He was all alone in the cold and he was crying. He looked so . . . hopeless.

"No," I say again. "It's nothing like that." *Please don't let it be anything like that.* "He's just a really private person. And anyway, he's pretty well-adjusted. One of those naturally optimistic kind of people. It's kind of annoying, actually. I doubt he could be that way if he was getting abused on a regular basis." *Could he?*

"Maybe it's drugs," Jules says, wadding up the empty chip bag and tossing it, missing the trashcan by my bed.

Before I can answer that, Mojo starts barking his head off at the sound of the doorbell. Jules rolls off the bed.

"I'm outta here," she says. "Let me know if he figures out the kissing thing. Or if you find out he's a serial killer."

No one gets to read my book, he'd said. *Not until I kill the villain.* What did he mean by that?

I smack Jules on the back of the head.

"Stop it," I say. "The guy is entitled to his privacy."

She rubs her head and gives me a grudging look. "If he's got a closet full of assault rifles, don't say I didn't warn you."

When we get downstairs, I grab Mojo's collar as she opens the door. Devon is holding a large soda and he's draining the last of it from the gurgling sound it makes. He lets out a loud, satisfied *aaah* and then follows it up with a burp.

"Sexy," Jules remarks.

Devon looks only mildly ashamed. "Sorry. Had to finish washing down my burger."

"How much red meat can one man eat?" I ask, gesturing for him to come in.

Jules makes her way around him. "Nice seeing you again," she says, as she heads out the door. "Behave yourselves."

"Why? Are we planning a bank heist?" Devon asks.

"Her mom won't be home for hours, and her dad's out of town," Jules informs him. "It's just the two of you."

I give her a look. "Goodbye, Jules."

Devon waves and shoots me a crooked grin as I close the door. "She's not going to be hanging around peeking in the windows, is she?"

I grimace. "It's entirely possible with her."

"She does like to talk. I noticed that in class."

"You have *no* idea."

I let go of the dog's collar, and he runs right at Devon, sniffing and yipping and making a nuisance of himself. Devon drops down to his knees, scruffing up Mojo's ears as the dog's entire back end whips frantically back and forth.

"He's an excitable little guy. I love wiener dogs. You know they were bred to hunt badgers? Everybody's afraid of badgers except daschunds." He remarks. "What's his name?"

"Mojo."

"Mojo. I like it."

"My brother picked it out. I thought it was stupid at the time, but it suits him."

"It does," Devon says, then he lowers his voice, and in a guttural tone he rasps out: *"Guter hund!"*

"What the hell was that?"

"I'm learning German now. He's a dachshund, so I told him he's a good dog in German. I think."

Mojo wags even more enthusiastically, lapping up the attention. They're both adorable together. How could you think of Devon as anything but harmless?

I take a deep breath, refusing to let Jules's stupid words eat my brain. She's right about one thing. Devon and I are going to be alone in this house for at least the next four hours. I'm going to make the most of it. But first—

"I need your help with something," I tell him.

"Sure. Whatever you need."

"You have to help me put together glam kits for a birthday party full of nine and twelve year-old girls."

He looks confused. "Okay, not my normal, but I'm sure I can manage. Why didn't you ask Jules to help you?"

"Because she would ask too many questions," I sigh. "And then she'd run her mouth at school about it all day tomorrow. I kind of want to keep this on the down-low."

"A mysterious, secret girly glam party," he says, putting his empty soda cup down on a nearby table and rubbing his hands together. "Sounds exciting."

I gesture for him to follow me and we walk through the house and into the garage.

"We'll start here," I say, pulling a large plastic bin off of one of the shelves built into the wall. I pop off the top and start pulling out the tote bags, purses, and wristlets, and arranging them by style and color group.

"That's an ugly purse," Devon says, holding up a large, rectangular zippered bag with multicolored flowers all over it.

"It's not a purse. It's a covered casserole tote."

"Who the hell carries around a casserole?"

"People going to home parties where they can buy more crap to stick in their garage and drink a lot of wine, that's who. We only want this style," I say, holding up a smaller bag. "It's actually a lunchbox tote, but it's big enough to hold all the stuff we're going to cram into it. Now look for the girly ones."

He peers again into the container. "They're all girly. Manly men would not possess these items."

"You and your fragile masculinity can select eight of these and line them up for me—and make sure they're all different patterns."

He gives me a salute. "On it."

I yank another plastic tote down from a shelf and paw through it. "Let's see . . . skin toner, lengthening mascara—no, maybe not. Their moms might not let them wear makeup yet. We'll stick with the toner, some lip moisturizer, and—oh good! Nail wraps!"

I line them all up in groups of eight as I find them, and Devon steps over to take a look.

"Are those like peel and stick fingernails?" He asks.

"Yeah, but they're really pretty good quality. They last a couple of weeks, as long as you're not free solo climbing a rock wall or something."

"Damn," he says, snapping his fingers. "I was eyeballing that black-and-white checkerboard pattern, but I guess my active lifestyle won't support my need to be a trendsetter."

I pick up the nail wraps and toss them into the lunch totes one at a time. "These were trendy two years ago. That's why they're out here with the clearance items. Start grabbing things and stuffing them in."

He reaches for the skin toner as I grab another bin, lift the lid, then close it up and slide it back on the shelf.

"This one's got diet shakes. No good."

"Don't want them starting early with the body issues," he agrees. He tosses the last tube of toner in. "What now?"

"Um . . . let's try this one."

I gesture toward a large container on the top shelf and he reaches over me to pull it down.

"Holy guacamole," he says as I lift the lid. "It looks like Disney threw up in there."

"They're leggings—just the patterns that didn't sell well," I say. "We'll pull out any that are small or extra small. Maybe grab a couple of mediums and larges. I'll give her extra since I don't know the sizes of the girls."

"How come I never see you wear these?"

"I'm not a crazy patterns kind of girl. I do have a couple pairs of straight black."

"For when you channel your inner Goth?"

"No, because they go with everything, smartass."

Devon starts to reach for a large red bin on the middle shelf, and my hand shoots out to stop him.

"No. Not those."

"Are they too ugly to be worn?" He asks, his face frozen in mock horror.

Heat floods my cheeks. "It's too—adult. My mom used to sell adult products at home parties."

His eyes go wide. "Seriously? I've *got* to look now."

He opens the lid on the bin and lets out a low whistle. "*God.* They're in all sizes. And colors! Not much variety in girth, though."

I shoot him a deadpan look. "Please."

"Maybe they should team up with the leggings people and offer some crazy patterns," he suggests as he puts the bin back and grabs a lunch tote.

"I'll put you in touch with their marketing rep."

"See that you do." He holds out the lunch tote, so that I can throw in some aromatherapy cream.

I tap my chin, thinking for a moment before I point. "That heavy bin on the bottom—grab it. That's got all kinds of funky soap."

"Funky?"

I pop the lid off and hold one up for him to smell. "They're samples for the soap making kits. They have the basic stuff like lavender and generic floral, but they also have silly stuff like this one."

He takes a deep whiff. "It kinda smells like bananas."

"That's why they call it Monkey Farts," I say, flipping the bar over so he can look at the label on the plastic wrap.

"Monkey Farts. I like it. Can I keep one? I promise to rub it all over my hot bod and think of you."

The mental picture slides into my head and the resulting heat makes my cheeks redden again. I pull down another bin filled with scented candles and wax melts and start unloading.

"So," Devon says, packing as he talks. "You haven't told me who you're doing this for."

"You'll keep it secret?"

He mimes locking his lips and throwing away a key.

"Maya Rodriguez," I explain. "Her sisters have birthdays close together this weekend, and Maya's mom has to work extra hours at their store, so it's on Maya to put the entire party together."

"She told you all that? Without throwing a punch?"

"I'm sure it crossed her mind," I say grimly. "She just seemed really stressed and I felt like I should—like I ought to—help. I mean, my mom has all this stuff and it's just gathering dust here. I can get rid of it for her, and all Maya has to do is make the cake."

Devon breaks into a wide grin. "That's insanely nice of you."

"I didn't do it to be nice," I snap.

He raises his hands. "Don't bite my head off for telling you that you did a nice thing. I'm just saying."

"Well I'm not doing it to try and butter her up or anything. We are not going to be buddies. It just seemed like somebody should help her. Help them."

I have no idea why, but tears sting my eyes. Devon reaches out and his fingers trail over my cheek, keeping me from turning away. His eyes lock with mine and before I can take a breath, he moves in, pressing me into the containers on the shelf behind me, and his lips are on mine.

The kiss is slow, sweet and searching—like he's trying to figure me out, learn what I like. And I like this. Oh, do I like this.

My lips part as his tongue traces their seam, and the kiss deepens. My hands slide up and into his silky-soft hair, gripping fistfuls as this kiss goes on and the heat of his body is seeping into mine. I groan low in my throat, and he answers with a groan of his own, shifting to push even tighter into me, rocking the shelves behind me. A loud *whump!* startles us both as a container crashes to the ground, spilling technicolor phalluses and edible underwear at our feet.

I stare at the pile, stunned. Devon barks a laugh. "I promised you a spectacular first kiss, didn't I?"

I laugh, too. Loud. And I can't stop. I'm snorting with laughter, which makes Devon howl and that makes me laugh even more.

"That's got to be the most ridiculous first kiss in history," I manage to gasp out.

"I'll get these cleaned up." He says. "Whoa! Look how far some of them bounced!"

"I'll grab more Monkey Farts," I say, moving over to the soap bin. "Then we can head upstairs and raid the outdated costume jewelry and whatever else she has shoved into the guest room closet."

He clacks a couple of colorful products together. I laugh again.

"I love to hear you laugh," he tells me as he tosses them in the bin and reaches for two more. "I'm going to make it a personal mission to get you to do that more often."

"I've laughed more since I met you than I have in the last year," I tell him truthfully. I get up on my tiptoes and plant a peck on his cheek. "Thank you."

With a wicked grin, he tosses the phalluses over his shoulder, and reaches for me, kissing me once again.

I KNEW MONDAY was going to be a bad day as soon as Mom made me breakfast.

She likes to sleep in, and unless she's got an early meeting or product delivery that day, she's usually just getting up when I leave the house for school. I stayed up FaceTiming Devon really late last night and didn't take a shower before bed. My hair is an absolute nightmare if I skip a shower so I got myself up early and dealt with it. And I hate getting up early.

Mom was waiting for me in the kitchen, with two mugs of Green Bright Beginnings tea—which isn't as bad as chamomile—and a plate of really awful muffins that she baked with ingredients from this month's meal subscription box. They have so much granola in them they look like they're made of sticks and twigs, and they turn to sludge in your mouth, requiring multiple drinks of liquid to clear them from your throat. I make a face as I glance down at them.

"I don't have time for breakfast," I tell her.

"You don't have to be at school for another twenty-five minutes."

"Yeah, but I have to stop by and get Jules, and you know how she is. I'll probably have to wake her up." That's not entirely a lie—it's happened many times before. But I'm not taking Jules with me today. She's faking sick so she can finish her history paper, but Mom doesn't know that.

"Oh?" She says, cocking her head slightly to the side. "I thought you'd be riding with your new boyfriend. The one I have yet to meet. You had him over on Thursday and I thought he'd stay so you could introduce us."

"We were working on a project." That is also not entirely a lie. We honestly were packing those gift bags most of the time, with some incredibly hot kisses sprinkled in. I wasn't about to get him naked when my mom could walk through the door at any minute. Besides, he wasn't pushing for it anyway. Which makes me like him even more.

"You were out with him twice this last weekend. You couldn't have brought him in?" she persists. "It would've been nice to have met him."

"He had to get home after the movies, and you weren't home yesterday."

"Meredith says he's a neighborhood boy. He lives on her cul-de-sac."

"Yeah, over on Willow." Meredith is one of the neighborhood gossip squad who is also in my mom's downline. I sling my backpack over my shoulder and grab a couple of Pop Tarts out of the pantry.

"I gotta go."

"You'll have to get me in touch with his mother," she says. "What's his name again?"

"Devon. And I already asked him. His mom doesn't like selling stuff."

"Then I definitely need to talk to her, because what we do isn't selling. It's educating. It's *engaging*."

I hold up a hand. "Save the sales pitch. You're making me late."

"Blue, we need to talk."

I'm almost at the door. My hand is on the knob.

"It'll have to be later."

"After school, then." She calls out.

"Can't. I have detention with Mrs. Ramsey." I can't believe I'm suddenly grateful to be saying that, but I am. I open the door but before I can make my escape, she walks up behind me.

"I know you got a letter from Jack."

That freezes me in my tracks, and I slowly turn to see her holding the letter in her hand.

"You went in my *room*?" I ask in disbelief.

"I was looking for laundry," she says with an innocent shrug that I don't believe for one minute. "I recognized the handwriting, of course."

"On the letter? In my desk drawer? Which was closed?" I retort.

She glances down at the letter. "Well? Are you going to write him back?"

If I tell her no, it's going to be a whole big thing. If I tell her she's a nosey bitch, it will only get worse.

"Why are you snooping in my room?" I demand.

"You're not handling things very well, right now!" She actually raises her voice, waving the letter in the air. "Secret boyfriends, fights at school, I have no idea what's really going on in your life!"

"No, you don't!" I shout back.

We stare at each other a long moment, both of us breathing hard from the spike in blood pressure. I don't have the time or mental room for this discussion.

"I'll talk to Jack when I'm ready. I'm still thinking about what I want to say."

"Why don't you start with 'I was glad to hear from you and I miss you'?"

"I have to go."

"Bl—"

I shut the door before she can even finish my one syllable name. Snooping in my room! She was probably looking for signs that Devon and I were using her adult products on each other.

My fuming gives way to a moment of panic as I start my car, wondering if maybe she had some specific way of stacking those adult products in that bin. Could she tell that we had been in there? I'm trying to figure out if I find that humorous or mortifying. Probably a little of both.

Mom went for that letter because she knew that Jack had written to me because she told him to. I mean, she ordered him to call me, and when I wouldn't pick up, she ordered him to write me, too.

Why does she have to push so hard? Of course I miss Jack. I miss him a lot. I wish he was here so I could punch his stupid face. Repeatedly.

And when I'm done with that, I'll wait in fear to see what sort of horrible prank he plays on me in retaliation. He'd probably post a really ugly picture of me online or something—catch me sleeping with my mouth open, or video me dancing with Mojo.

I smile a little bit at the memory. I was dancing Mojo around the room, bobbing up and down with the beat—badly, because I can't dance. Jack startled me when he ran in screaming that he was recording me and I squeezed Mojo a little too hard. He ended up peeing on me. All of that caught on video, of course. Jack posted it right away. People were passing me in the hall school the next day making sniffing sounds, and asking me if I wanted to borrow some perfume or if I needed a puppy pad. It was really shitty of him.

Good times—when that was the shittiest thing I had to deal with in a school day.

As I drive to school, my mind keeps returning to Jack. I bet he's wishing for a good old shitty school day too.

I don't have any friends here, and none of my friends back at home visit. I think they're afraid for anyone to know they have contact with me. Like I've got a disease or something.

I know things are awful for him, but that disease is contagious. They stare at me because they can't stare at him right now. They stare at me because I share a building six and a half hours a day with the other girl who caught the same disease from him. And we're all stuck in our respective lives.

If only Jack hadn't gone to that party. If only he hadn't tried to drive home. If he had just been five minutes later on that damn road, or five minutes earlier. I can wish all I want for *if* but I know it's useless. Jack knows it's useless, too.

After I punch his stupid face, I really want to hug him.

I'M STILL NOT in the best mood when Mrs. Linza tells us to pair up and rehearse talking about our chosen books with each other. She seems to think this will help with our presentations, giving us the practice of re-telling the story to someone.

I pair up with Devon, and we push our desks to the back corner of the classroom. Like I said, I'm already in a bad mood. I really don't want to do this. Luckily for me, Devon has his usual level of enthusiasm.

"So it's a book about a seagull?" I ask, letting my disinterest show. "He eats garbage off the boardwalk and craps all over people. It doesn't sound terribly exciting to me."

Devon leans back in his chair, clasping his hands behind his head. "Ah, but that's where you're wrong. Jonathan Livingston Seagull is about the soul."

I look at him with dead eyes. "The soul of a seagull. A rat with wings."

"That's the beauty of the story. Who would think for one second about trying to get inside the mind of a seagull? They eat, they poop, they sleep, and they reproduce. Basic animal functions—or bird functions. But this book?" He taps his finger on the cover of the book, sitting in front of him on the desk. "This book shows you what it means to *fly*. To really challenge yourself. To open yourself to all the possibilities in your life."

"As told by a seagull."

"As told *about* a seagull. Jonathan is no ordinary seagull. He wants to be more. So he pushes himself to get just the right angle on his wings, just the right curvature on the tips, pushing his limits to go just a little bit faster, just a little bit higher. He fails a lot before he accomplishes it, and even gets kicked out of his flock for being a non-conformist, but he becomes the best at flying. And then he gets even better than that. It goes all existential—I won't spoil it for you, but it's some deeply philosophical stuff."

"Carpe diem? Or the seagull equivalent?"

"Exactly." He thumps the book again. "Squeeze every single second out of your life. Toss aside all the stuff that's bogging you down and holding you back. Push forward and fly higher."

I dictate out loud as I write in the notebook in front of me: *"Should be preserved as the foundation of a new religion based on garbage-eating scavenger fowl."*

He smiles at me. "Okay, I get that it sounds ridiculously life—affirming, but it really is a good book."

"You sound like you're about to sell me a line of diet shakes."

I look over my shoulder, and Mrs. Linza is bent over a student, talking to them about their book. I dig in my backpack and pull out a paperback, setting it on my desk. "Speaking of that—"

"*Mindfulness Over Madness: Your Guide to Self-Realization Through Negation Release*," Devon reads. "*This* is your book?"

"It's one of my mom's. I had to grab something. Should be easy to talk about."

His brow crinkles in surprise. "You don't have a favorite book?"

"I have a few," I say defensively. "I've been so busy with school and work. I haven't read a lot lately."

"There's got to be at least one book you can think of," he says.

I feel my cheeks go slightly red. "I like to read romance," I say, dropping my voice down so nobody hears me. "Not like, all the time, just as an escape."

He reaches across and puts his hand over mine. "I don't know why you're embarrassed about that. Books are a great escape. You like to escape into love stories. That's no less valid than escaping into a horror story or a sci-fi story, or a story about a seagull who wants to break the sound barrier before he poops out all the french fries he ate on the beach today."

"I'm not going to talk about a romance story."

He holds up his hands. "Just a thought. So tell me about *Mindfulness over Madness*. What makes it worth preserving after civilization falls?"

"It's going to enable me to step forward confidently into my best life," I say, with faux fervency. "And if I can empower women to walk a mile in my patterned leggings before embracing their inner boss-babe-radiant-skinned warrior, maybe we can all share a spirulina shake and change the world."

He gives me an incredibly earnest look as he grabs his notebook and opens it. "I am intrigued by your premise, and would like to subscribe to your newsletter," he says, placing his hand over his heart.

"This brave new world will be our downline. Write that down." I tap his notebook with my pen, and then I notice the drawing on the open page. It's a woman's face—I think. But in some weird, very colorful pattern.

"That's interesting. Is it for Graphic Arts?"

"Nope, just for fun," he says. "It's your face but you probably don't recognize it with the pattern. I borrowed the idea from one of those pairs of leggings."

"You gave me legging face?" I didn't realize I said that so loud until Mrs. Linza's head turns in our direction.

"Blue? Devon?" She strolls over as Devon casually flips the notebook page and starts writing notes. "How's it coming along?" she asks.

"Good," I lie. "Really good. I'm going to empower what's left of our fallen civilization, and Devon is going to discuss the psychology of seagulls."

She glances down at our books. "Jonathan Livingston Seagull is a favorite of mine," she says to him. He gives me a smug look, riding high on her validation. Then her gaze moves over to my book.

"Looks like you're interested in self-help," she says. Her fingers reach out and rest lightly on my shoulder. "That's a positive step for you, Blue."

And just like that, my lousy mood that had started to improve goes right back to lousy again. Everybody in the class is looking at me because they were all expecting her to come down on us for goofing off. Instead, she makes it sound like I'm badly in need of my mother's crappy empowerment book. I want to throw it at her.

"She didn't mean anything by it," Devon whispers after she moves away.

"Sure she did," I grumble. "I'm the psycho sister of the guy who drives around killing people, haven't you heard? I punch teachers and suppress minorities and I need all the help I can get."

"It's not like that."

I don't bother to answer. The bell rings, so I cram my book into my backpack and walk out. Devon puts his hand on my arm when we get out into the hallway, stopping me.

"*I* don't see you like that."

"I know you don't," I say with a sigh. "See you at lunch."

I walk fast down the hallway, so he won't notice me blinking back the tears. My nerves are on a ragged edge today, and the tiniest thing is going to push me over. I feel like everybody is staring at me. I feel like I'm a bad sister, and a bad girlfriend, because Devon is being his usual wonderful and supportive self, and I spent half the night last night wondering what sort of dark secrets he's still keeping from me.

It's like I can't even let myself be happy about the one good thing going in my life. Maybe I read romance because it's as close as I'll ever get to a happily ever after.

Jules catches up with me just before third block. We've got an assembly today—Theatre Arts club is doing a showcase of songs from the upcoming spring musical. It also gives them a chance to advertise their Valentine's Day fundraiser—singing telegrams.

"I mean it," Jules says. "I'm going to wear a red shirt and blend right in with all of them as they deliver their singing telegrams. Then I'm going to start screaming death metal in people's faces."

"You are *not* right," I say, shaking my head.

"I can alternate between *Maggot Dreams* and *Anal Anarchy*," she suggests.

"I would pay cash money to see that."

"I know, right?"

We slide into our seats in the auditorium, choosing the back so we can talk as the chorus takes the stage.

"So—still together?"

I turn my head to glare at Jules. She's asked me that question every day since Devon and I got together.

"Yes. Stop asking me that."

"Has he let you inside his secret abode?"

"He's Batman now?"

"You tell me." She looks at the performers on the stage. "I hate this song."

"What is it?"

"I don't know. But I hate it. Did you and Maya decide on a club?"

"No. We didn't get anywhere last time. Mrs. Ramsey had us discussing our hobbies, so we can find a shared passion," I say with a good deal of disgust.

"Don't you already have one of those? Though what either one of you see in Austin I'll never know. He always has sweat stains on his underarms."

"He plays football," I remind her.

"Every minute of the day? The boy's never heard of antiperspirant?"

"Well, now Maya and I have two things in common," I say. "He's her ex, too."

Jules turns her head to look at me. "Wait—they broke up?"

"You didn't know that?" For once I know something that Jules doesn't know. This has to be a first.

"Who told you?" She demands.

"Maya did. She says he's boring. And she's right."

I guess I didn't realize it before, because I didn't have much to hold him up against. I haven't had the greatest track record with boyfriends—until recently. I am never bored with Devon. Never.

Jules's entire face crinkles into one giant question mark. "Wait—you're talking to Maya?"

"Sort of," I say uncomfortably. "I mean, not like we're friends or anything. She just kind of mentioned it."

"When you were talking." Jules is staring at me now.

"She just made a comment, that's all."

"So I guess the great afterschool detention experiment is working, then." She looks at the stage again. "You know, I think I hate this song more."

"It's bad."

"Her voice is totally wrong for it."

"Totally."

Jules slinks down in her seat and closes her eyes, clearly intending to nap through the rest of the assembly. I look around the auditorium, and see Maya talking to Haylee, sitting on the other side and a few rows ahead of me. I wonder how the weekend went. If her sisters had a good time at their party. I hope so.

So yeah, the great afterschool detention experiment isn't a total bust.

Devon pushes his way down our row, and flops into the empty space on the other side of me. He leans in to give me a quick kiss on the cheek before he says:

"Man, I love this song."

He takes my hand, threading our fingers together and I think to myself, *maybe this year is looking up.*

Mood: officially improved.

"MRS. RAMSEY IS ill today, girls," Mrs. Logan says brusquely. "I have a parent meeting, so I won't be able to step in for her. I'm afraid we're going to have to reschedule today's session."

"Great," I grumble. "We get to stretch it out even longer."

"Waste of time," I hear Maya say as I'm walking toward the door. I don't realize she's following me until I get out to the far parking lot—the only spot I could find this morning because Jules overslept and made us late. Maya calls my name as I'm unlocking my door, and I jump because she's right behind me.

"Shit! You scared me."

She holds out a grocery bag. "Here," she says.

I take it from her, and a frown creases my brow as I look inside and see two of the goody bags that Devon and I put together for her party, as well as the extra pairs of leggings.

"You didn't have to give me back the leftovers," I tell her. "If somebody didn't show or whatever, your sisters can keep the stuff. How'd it go?"

"These *are* my sister's bags," she bites out. "You left one of your mother's business cards inside that inner pocket. My mom found it and had a total meltdown."

My mouth goes dry. "Oh my God. Maya—I'm sorry!"

"Yeah, I'll bet you are. Was this your way of getting back at me?" She demands. "Using me to slap my mother in the face? Was it fun for you to imagine her screaming at my sisters, throwing the bags up against the wall? Did you enjoy that?" Her fury makes her voice crack on that last question.

"I didn't—Maya, I didn't know!" Dammit, why didn't I check? Why didn't I check the bags? I should've known Mom would do that!

"My mother spent the rest of the night crying in her bedroom," Maya snarls. "So thanks again for giving my sisters a really memorable birthday. You must be so proud—attacking me and hurting a couple of kids who never did anything to you."

"Maya, it was a mistake. I didn't—"

"Save it." She throws her hand up dismissively and turns to walk away. I grab her shoulder and spin her around to face me. She knocks my hand away.

"I was trying to help you," I remind her. "I didn't know my mother put her damn business card in there. I wouldn't have done that on purpose! And while we're at it, who are you to talk about attacking someone who never did anything to you?"

"Don't even go there! Your family screwed us all over *hard*, and you know it!"

"I had nothing to do with any of that! I wasn't in that car!"

"You were in the courtroom! You were hugging your brother when your Daddy's fancy lawyer got him out of a manslaughter charge!"

"In case you forgot," I snarl, pointing my finger right in her face. "Your mother agreed to the plea bargain. I wonder why that was? Probably because her lawyer knew she didn't have a case!"

Maya suddenly, spectacularly implodes.

"Bitch!" She screams, but it's more like a wail. Then she shoves me, hard. "Bitch!" She screams it again and punches the side of my car. I jump back, startled, as she keeps on punching, punctuating with a word for every punch.

"I! Hate! You! I! Hate! You!"

She flips around, covers her face with her hands and slides down the car to the ground. Her hand is a bloody mess, and she's crying, great gulping sobs that shake her body.

I stand there helplessly watching her, glancing around to see if anyone else is seeing this, but it looks like we are alone for the moment. What do I do? I don't know what to do. I know I'm not making it any better by standing here staring at her.

Finally, I sit down next to her, leaving a foot of space between us. There isn't anything to be said to make this better, so I don't say anything. I just unzip my backpack and find the stupid zippered pouch with the fluorescent floral designs on it that my mother gave me. It's got Advil, alcohol wipes, Band-Aids, and a pack of tissues in it. I pull out a few of the tissues and hand them over to Maya. She takes them without a word and holds them on her eyes as she struggles to get ahold of herself. Finally, she blows her nose and takes a few deep breaths.

"My mother took the plea bargain," she says in a very quiet voice, "because they had the transcripts of my dad's text messages. If we had continued the trial, they would've introduced them as evidence that he had been texting close to the time of the accident."

"I know."

"You *don't* know," she says, swiping at her eyes again with the tissues. "My dad was texting his girlfriend. My mom didn't know he was cheating on her. She couldn't bear the thought of everyone seeing those texts. Of everyone knowing."

She takes another deep breath in, but it breaks on a ragged sob as she puts her face in her hands again and cries, "How could he do that? How could he do that to her? To us?"

My shock renders me mute as Maya cries. And cries.

"Do—do your sisters know?" I finally ask.

She shakes her head and cries more, so I guess she was the only one her mother told. One more burden she has to bear.

"I'm sorry." It's all I can seem to say. "God, Maya, I'm so sorry. Sorry this happened to you. To all of you."

She doesn't say anything, just keeps on crying. It's possible I'm the only one she's told. Haylee would tell everybody. Maya can tell me because she doesn't give a shit what I think about her. I watch her cry, feeling helpless and useless and so awful.

I'm an awful person. It all wells up inside me and then I say it.

"He tried to call me that night. Jack."

The words come out, like I ripped a Band-Aid off a wound and tore the scab with it. Now it's oozing, and it's all coming out.

"He tried to call me that night before he left the party," I go on. "I ignored him. I ignored his text, too. I fell asleep, and I had my ringer off—"

Now I'm crying. "I don't know what he wanted. I never asked him. He might've been trying to find somebody to pick him up. I don't know. I'm sorry. I'm so sorry."

I curl into a ball, setting my forehead on my knees and I'm crying, crying, crying. I feel her hand touch my shoulder, and before I know it, we're hugging each other fiercely, sobbing, the floodgates jammed wide open, washing over us both.

Eventually, we both pull back, rubbing at our eyes. I wipe my nose on my sleeve, and Maya reaches down and grabs the tissues, handing them to me.

"You need them more than me."

I give a watery laugh, and cram a few tissues on my nose, blowing hard.

"Sorry," I say again.

She pulls in a breath, let it out slowly. "I guess we both got a shitty deal."

"You got it worse."

She tips her head back to rest it against the car. "Yeah, I did."

"Do you know her?" I ask hesitantly. "The woman?"

"No. Our coffee shop is right by the train station. I think she was a regular customer. Whoever she was, she doesn't come in anymore." She turns her head and looks at me. "Your brother really texted you that night?"

"Yeah. All he said was 'Hey.' I guess when I didn't answer that's when he tried to call. I should have picked up."

We sit there in silence for a few moments, just breathing. Collecting ourselves.

"It's cold out here," Maya finally says. She holds out her hand, trying to flex the fingers.

"I've got stuff to clean you up." I pull out the alcohol pads and the Band Aids. "Does it feel broken?"

She flexes her fingers again and rotates her wrist. "No, I don't think so. Hurts like a bitch. Writing is going to suck for a while."

I watch as she dabs at her hand with the alcohol wipes, and I help her put on a couple of Band-Aids. They don't stick very well on her knuckles.

"Are you going to be able to play basketball?"

"I'll make it work," she says. She puts her injured hand down to the ground to push up, then winces when she tries to put weight on it. I get up to my feet and put a hand down. She grasps it with her good hand, and I pull her up.

"What time is it?" she asks.

I check my phone. "Almost four." I glance around the empty student parking lot. "Is somebody coming for you?"

"No. I was going to text Haylee and have her come get me." She glances down at her bruised and bandaged hand. "She's going to be all over me asking about this."

"I can give you a ride."

She gives me a look, but I go on. "I'll drop you a block away from home so your mom won't know it was me."

She considers a moment and flexes her hand again. "She's at work. And I'd appreciate it."

I open the car door for her, and she slides in. As I climb in the other side she pulls down the visor to check her face in the mirror on the back. I do the same.

"Ugh," she says.

"We're both pretty wrecked," I agree. "I've got some concealer and mascara in my backpack," I reach back to pull it up, handing it to her. "Second zipper."

She gives me directions to her house and awkwardly makes the repairs to her face—using her bad hand—as I navigate traffic. It turns out she only lives about ten miles from the school.

"What are you going to tell your mom about your hand?" I ask her.

"I'll tell her I tripped or something, I guess."

"You can tell her you hit me. She'd probably be okay with that."

Maya cracks a smile. "Yeah, probably. But then school would expel us both if they heard we were fighting."

She points to a bank on the corner of an upcoming street. "Turn here," she says. "The one on the end."

I pull into a townhouse community in a nice area. Maya's house has flower boxes on the windows and one of those colorful mailbox covers—this one for Valentine's Day. There's a decorative wreath on the front door. It looks like a nice place to live.

"Let me guess," Maya says. "Not what you were expecting."

"I thought you lived in the city."

"You thought I lived in Philly?"

"I guess I just assumed—"

"You just assumed that I lived in the hood? Right?"

"I just—no—you just seem like a city girl."

"Urban," she says, making finger quotes in the air. "That's the word you're looking for when you want to say somebody's from the hood but you don't want to sound like you're being racist while you say it."

"That's not what I meant."

"Your friend Olivia lives in Philly," she reminds me. "A beautiful townhouse off Rittenhouse Square—at least that's what she tells everybody. But because her daddy has a contract with King Limo to drive her here and pick her up every day in a luxury sedan, it's a different kind of Philly. I mean there's Philly and then there's *Philly*, right? Do you even realize how you sound?"

My next protest stalls on my lips. No, I didn't realize. But I didn't mean any of that. She's reading stuff into it and pinning it on me and that's pissing me off.

"I'm not a racist." I say, hating how defensive I sound. "And I can't help it if I'm rich."

"You're not rich. Your daddy is rich. You're just along for the ride. And I didn't use the word racist, but you're feeling it aren't you?"

The look she gives me makes me want to squirm.

"Look, I know we've got very different lives—"

"But we don't," she says, her hand cutting through the air. "Yeah, my parents came here from Puerto Rico, but I was born here. We live in a regular house in the suburbs. My Dad used to work a lot, too. We drive cars and eat out and shop at the mall. But everybody likes it better when we live *different lives* so we don't have to be included in theirs."

"I just meant I know I've never had to deal with some of the stupid shit you've had to deal with from people like me." She rolls her eyes, so I add: "Or from me directly. I don't always know how things come across."

She's not letting me off. "Sometimes you do know, though."

I swallow the uncomfortable tightness in my throat. "Sometimes I do—I *did*. And I'm sorry. I really am."

Maya's not looking away, holding me to every word of that. "So?" she finally says.

"If I say something—wrong—or insensitive, I want you to let me know."

I get a flat stare for a response.

"I mean it. I need to train myself to think about this stuff. So tell me. I won't be pissed."

"You're pissed right now."

I start to protest and she holds a hand up. "Okay. I'll call you out, when you need it." She puts the makeup back in my backpack and sets it in the back seat.

"Thanks for the ride," she says.

"Maya—I'm sorry. I really am. About . . . everything."

"I know." She gets out of the car, but pauses before she closes the door. She leans in.

"Hey," she says. "I don't really hate you. I just hate . . . all this shit."

"Me, too."

"Bye."

"Bye."

I watch her walk into the house, flexing and unflexing her hand as she goes.

I don't really know Maya Rodriguez. But I understand her a little more. Part of me wonders if we could have been friends before all this happened but I know that would have only made things so much worse.

"ALL OUR HARD work ruined," Devon tells me. "It makes sense your mom would put a business card in the bag, but I didn't even think about it. I'm sorry Maya ripped you a new one."

We're down in the basement, which is like a second family room. My dad intended it to be a man cave with hardwood floors, finished walls and ceiling, pool table, home theater system, and even a bar. We hardly ever use it. When Jack and I were younger we used to have parties with the neighbors, and people from my dad's work all the time. Now it's maybe three times a year, and Dad's too busy to come down here any other time. He did forbid mom to put any of her stuff down here, so at least I don't have to worry about knocking over a bin full of vibrators.

"Can you blame her?" I reply. "Her mother lost it on her."

"So, is she going to be blasting you on Instagram, or poisoning your food at school tomorrow?"

"Neither. She calmed down and we both apologized. I think we're okay."

I didn't tell him the rest of what Maya told me. I'm pretty sure I can trust him with a secret, but it isn't my secret to tell. No one else needs to be aware that she's got more going on.

I can't even begin to know what it's like for her. She's mourning her father, but now she's mourning the image she always had of him. She's struggling to reconcile what she's learned with the man she knew and loved. On top of that, she has to witness her mother's struggle, and all the fallout from that. The final cherry on top of that suck-ass cupcake is the fact that she can't get the justice she feels her father deserved because her mother went for the plea bargain to keep other people from learning the truth.

I try to imagine my father cheating on my mother. I suppose he could, and easily. He travels a lot. If my dad was stupid enough to do that, my mom would almost certainly find out. She's got her nose in everything. I have no doubt she would make his life a living hell if something like that went down.

But imagining that makes me feel sick. I don't want to, so I won't.

Devon starts to reach for the bowl of microwave popcorn on the table in front of him, then changes his mind.

"What?" I ask. "You don't want popcorn?"

He puts two fingers on his chin and rubs thoughtfully. "I'm thinking chips. What have you got?"

"At the moment?" I make a face. "All we have are some baked kale chips flavored with rosemary. My mom made them and they're sitting in a big bag in the cupboard. Even she won't eat them, but it took her two hours to make them so she won't throw them away."

"You don't have any potato chips? No Cheetos or Fritos?"

"Mom doesn't buy that stuff very often," I tell him. "Mostly Jack bought it."

I smile a little, remembering the P.S. Jack put in his letter.

I told somebody here about the Frito theory, and he agreed with us.

"Frito theory," I mumble.

"What?"

"Frito theory—it's something Jack and I came up with. Do you have a dog?"

"We have a cat. But that doesn't mean you and I aren't fated to be together." He reaches out and squeezes my hand. "We can overcome this."

I smile and shake my head. "I was asking because Jack and I both agree that dog paws smell like Fritos."

He looks at me for a moment as though he's sure I'm joking. "I demand proof."

"You want to smell Mojo's paws?"

"Well, you *are* my girlfriend now," he says. "Consider it a bonding experience."

I walk to the bottom of the stairs, and call Mojo's name, making kissing sounds, until he finally shows up and bounds down the stairs to me. I pick him up and walk him over to Devon, flipping him on his back to give easy access to his paws.

"He didn't just come in from outside or anything, did he?" Devon asks. "I mean, you're not setting me up for a really nasty smell, are you?"

"I'm not, I promise."

He gently takes Mojo's front paw between his fingers and starts to lean in, then he stops and looks up at me again.

"You understand that for the sake of science, I would need to smell multiple dog paws, so that we can adequately describe it as an overall dog phenomenon versus something that occurs only in *your* dog."

"Yes, but—"

"And we're not going to be able to learn if it's a cat phenomenon," he says, still holding Mojo's paw. "Cats use their feet to bury their poop in the litter box—that they also pee in. I'm not smelling their paws."

"That's nasty."

"Maybe we could gather some test subjects—"

"Will you just smell his paw already?" I ask impatiently. Mojo is not thrilled with laying on his back so long when there are no belly rubs involved. Devon finally leans in, and takes a cautious sniff. Then he leans back and gives me an odd look.

"I honestly thought you were kidding me."

I put Mojo down and he scampers over to Devon to get his ears rubbed.

"Frito theory," I say again. "And for the record, it's not isolated to my dog only. You can Google it. There's some kind of weird bacteria that makes their feet smell like corn chips."

Devon reaches for the bowl of popcorn. "Okay, you and your brother may have just put me off Fritos for a very long time."

"I'll be sure to tell Jack the next time I talk to him."

"How much longer has he got?"

"I don't know—around four months, I think?"

"Have you seen him since Christmas?" Devon tosses a piece of popcorn in the air for Mojo. He catches it, and Devon applauds.

"They didn't let him come home for Christmas. My mom was seriously pissed and let the program director have it."

"Did you smuggle a turkey dinner under your coat for him?"

I shift uncomfortably. "I didn't go," I say in a small voice.

Devon stares at me in surprise, his lips slightly parted. Finally, he reaches for more popcorn and crams it in his mouth, almost like he is doing it because he doesn't know what to say.

"I was really tired. I wanted to sleep in. And it's not like we could really do anything anyway," I defend. "They only let my parents see him for two hours, and they had a big Christmas meal for everybody there—he had to help cook it. I bought him a present, and Mom gave it to him, along with all the other stuff they gave him."

"Mmm-hmm," is all that Devon says as he keeps on chewing.

"They had to bring all the presents home. They wouldn't let him keep them there. But the program gave him the day off from everything he normally has to do, and they even let them all watch movies."

I have a lump in my throat. I don't know why I have a lump in my throat. Why do I feel like I have to defend myself? *Because you should have been there*, a little voice says inside my head.

"Do you think I'm a bad sister?" I ask Devon.

He shakes his head immediately. "No. If you were a bad sister, you wouldn't feel so awful about what you just told me. But you love your brother, so you do."

"It's just that—oh, I don't know what it is," I sink down on the couch next to him. "I'm still so angry at him for derailing his own life. For wrecking Maya's life. For making my life harder than it has to be at school, and for leaving me home alone with my parents while we all deal with this."

Devon puts his arm around me and pulls me close to his side. He stays quiet for a while, just holding me.

"Your brother made a bad choice," he says softly. "Part of you feels like you're having to pay for it, too. That's not easy for you, or your parents."

He kisses the top of my head, and I sigh.

"Please tell me your family is as dysfunctional as mine," I beg him.

"I don't think your family's so bad," he says. "Your dad seems to like me. So does Mojo."

"Dad is easy. He's too busy to notice if you're a serial killer. You're lucky Mom isn't home. She's going to have a spreadsheet full of information on you so she can personalize your sales plan and all the inspirational quotes she'll give you."

"Sounds scary."

"I told you—utterly dysfunctional."

"Every family is dysfunctional on some level," he says. "And you guys are dealing with something that most people don't have to deal with. Cut yourself a break."

"Does your family—" I break off at the realization. "I haven't really asked about your family."

"It's okay," he says. "You've been completely dazzled by me. It's understandable."

I reach up, and give his beanie a tug down over his eyes. He shoves it back in place and then he leans down to kiss me. I let him, but push against his chest before he can deepen it.

"I'm serious," I say. "You haven't told me much."

"My dad works in cybersecurity for a pharmaceutical company. My mom is a nurse."

He looks like he wants to say something else about them but then he pauses a moment before he grins and says: "My cat is inherently evil, and farts in bed at night."

"What's his name?"

"Bill."

I give him a look. "Yes, the name just reeks of evil."

"It's always the mundane that disguises the true evil beneath." He reaches for another handful of popcorn, and stuffs his mouth full again. I guess that means he doesn't want to talk anymore, but I'm determined to learn more.

"Anything else? I feel like you know all about me and I've barely scratched the surface with you."

"My parents met at the beach," he says, grabbing more popcorn. "What about yours?"

"Huh." I think for a moment. "I really don't know."

"You never asked?"

"They met at college, but I don't know exactly where. Probably in a class or at a party. And you're changing the subject. We are talking about you."

He lets out a heavy sigh. "Do we have to? I'm just not that interesting."

"I want to know how you got this." I reach up and push his hair back, exposing the bruise on his forehead. "Did you think I wouldn't notice?"

He smooths his hair back down, his face scrunching up when his fingers brush the bruise. "I was hoping you wouldn't," he says. "Got it by being a dumb-ass. I tripped down the stairs and hit the railing with my head on the way down."

"Seriously?"

"Tripped over the cat, if you want the specifics." He smiles. "Which is oddly appropriate because we named him Bill for the movie *Kill Bill*. And Bill was an assassin."

"So you have parents who met at the beach, and a cat that's trying to kill you."

He spreads his hands wide. "See, that's all you need to know about my life story today."

"Today?" I have to push a little more. "Maya saw you at the hospital. Right before we started dating."

He freezes momentarily as he reaches for another handful of popcorn, then takes his time putting it in his mouth and chewing before he shrugs. "I'm fine. It wasn't anything like she's making it out to be. Do we have to talk about this? I'd rather talk about you. You're my favorite subject." He holds a smile but it's tight. Forced.

"Not that I mind having you over at my house," I say, giving up the inquest—for now. "But I'd like to meet your parents sometime."

He nods, chewing on his popcorn until he clears his mouth. "You will. It's just that things are a little hectic for them right now. Catch!"

He leans back with a piece of popcorn balanced between his thumb and forefinger. I open my mouth and he tosses it. It misses and drops down the front of my shirt right into my bra.

"You did that on purpose!"

He waggles his eyebrows and gives me an evil grin. I laugh, digging the kernel out and then he motions me to toss it back at him. He catches it on the first try.

"Best popcorn I ever ate," he says, smacking his lips together.

"Guess it's a good thing we weren't eating Fritos and bean dip."

"That would be far from romantic."

My finger traces a pattern on his knee. "Speaking of romance . . ."

He shifts closer, and his eyes get that look—the one that makes my pulse start to pound. I resist the urge to lean in.

"Valentine's Day is next week and you still haven't told me what I can get you."

His answer is a leer.

"Seriously," I laugh. "I have no idea what to get you for a present. I mean, do you have an Xbox? Or are you a PlayStation kind of guy?"

He leans back with a sigh. "Video games—the true path to a man's heart."

"I could cook for you, if you're into that."

"You can *cook*?" He sits up again like I poked him with something.

I give him a deadpan look. "I'm Italian. It's sort of required."

"Pasta?"

"I can make lasagna that'll have your eyes rolling back in your head, and my chicken piccata is nothing less than life-altering."

"How did I not know this about you?" He asks, clearly amazed.

"Now we're even," I tell him. "Only, not really. There's still tons of stuff I don't know about you."

"Later," he says softly. He draws me in and I'm breathless by the time his lips settle on mine.

He pulls me across his lap, his hand shifting slowly over my side and back while the fingers of the other hand twine in my hair. At the slow press of his mouth on mine, I dissolve, losing myself in the taste and smell and feel of him, in the heated slide of our tongues as they circle and dance, his lips moving on mine, sending delicious tingles down every nerve in my body. It's a long time before we come up for air.

And later, after I walk him to the door and we say goodnight, I replay our night in my head, every kiss, every stroke of his hands, every press of his fingers. The feel of his body on mine.

I still don't know much about him, but do I need to, really? Do I?

DEVON PICKS ME up for school on Valentine's Day, and there are a dozen roses on the seat next to him in the car.

"I figured I'd give them to you when I picked you up, so you could put them in the house and not have to carry them from class to class all day," he says. "Happy Valentine's Day."

"They're beautiful." I lean in to kiss his cheek before I walk them into the house and set them on the kitchen counter. Mom looks up from her Joyful Morning Exuberance tea and raises an eyebrow, but she doesn't say anything. Thank God.

On the drive to school, I can't help but remark.

"I wasn't expecting roses," I say. "They seem so—normal. For you, I mean."

"I can be a traditional sort of guy," Devon says defensively. "Roses are pretty. I like giving you pretty things."

I reach across and put my hand over his on the gearshift. "I love them, I really do."

"Well, it's not all I got you."

"It's more than enough. You didn't need to get me anything else. I'm just glad I have you."

His smile is blinding. "That's the nicest thing anyone's ever said to me."

"It's true."

"It's true for me, too. With you."

"I'm giving you my present later, with dinner."

"You didn't have to do that. Dinner is enough."

I grin. "I guess we both overdid."

He turns his hand over to interlace our fingers, giving my hand a squeeze. "No such thing for us."

After we slide into our desks in Mrs. Linza's class, I realize how serious he is about that. I reach down into my backpack to pull out my notebook, and when I raise back up again, there's a card on my desk. I glance over at him, and Devon is staring up at the ceiling and twiddling his thumbs in a circular motion, his face a study in exaggerated innocence. I snicker, unable to help myself.

As Mrs. Linza goes over the parameters again for the upcoming book presentation, I open the card.

It's a picture of a hamburger with a face drawn on it, and the eyes are hearts.

You're the only bun for me, it says inside. Also tucked inside is a keychain in the shape of an onion.

I shoot him a sideways glance. "Now that's more like it," I say under my breath. He leans back in his seat, clearly pleased with himself. The rest of the class passes as I fiddle with my new keychain.

As soon as the bell rings, I am out of my seat and kissing him quickly. "I love it," I say, and I mean it.

"It's an onion ring," he replies. "Get it?"

I hold it up, jingling it slightly. "Embrace your inner onion."

"Enjoy your day," he says with a mysterious smile.

Before I can ask him to elaborate, he's off like a shot.

I settle into my desk in Astronomy class when Matt Lewandowski walks over and drops a wrapped package in front of me.

"Your boyfriend paid me ten bucks to deliver this," he says unceremoniously before he walks away.

I stare at the box, hoping there's nothing breakable in there and rip it open quickly before Ms. Marquette starts class.

The box is full of candy. Starbursts. Milky Way bars. Mars bars. Orbit gum. A Valentine sits on top of the pile—one of those ones you get a pack in elementary school. It has pictures of stars and planets on it and in bright pink bubblegum letters it says: *Valentine, you are out of this world!*

I set the box down next to my chair, but not before I snag a pack of Starbursts to snack on during class.

I practically jog to the cafeteria because I want to see Devon— and that's a good thing, because I might as well apply his last gift directly to my ass. He's seated in the far corner at a table draped in a red tablecloth. A vase with a single rose stands at the center, and there are plates and plastic wine glasses set upon it.

Everyone in the cafeteria is staring at me now, and I take in the venue with wide eyes.

"What have you done?"

"I wanted us to dine in style," he says. He picks up a bottle. "Sparkling apple cider?"

He says that with an exaggerated British accent and it makes me laugh. Just like always. I slide into the chair across from him.

"You didn't have anything catered?" I reach for my wine glass, making sure to elevate my pinky.

"I thought about it," he confesses. "I couldn't figure out how to keep the food warm all day. So we'll eat their sub-par offerings, and pretend we're slumming it with the commoners."

"How very charitable of us."

"Isn't it, though?"

I glance over my shoulder toward the food line. "So what have they got today?"

"Vegetarian chili," he says with disgust. "I'm sticking with the salad bar. I need to eat light—got a big meal coming later."

"Yes, you do," I agree. "Four courses, plus dessert."

"Four courses?" His eyes widen with delight.

"Plus dessert." I give him a wicked, sultry look. He returns it, and adds a wink.

"I'll be thinking about that all day."

"That's my exact intention." My voice turns husky, and full of promise.

The school's chili isn't bad, but I limit myself to a small salad. Like Devon says, I've got a big meal coming later. And a hot date. A bowl full of beans is not a stellar idea.

Third block begins, and I nod to Maya as I take my seat. Twenty minutes into class, there's a knock at the door, and the Theater Arts club has arrived to deliver their singing telegrams.

I resist the urge to sink down in my chair as I wait, half in fear and half in excitement. My telegram is number three on their list. They break into a two-part harmony rendition of *A Whole New World* from *Aladdin*, surrounding my desk as my cheeks turn red and I stare at my metal onion.

As the song ends, one of them reaches behind their back and sets something on the desk in front of me. It's a square of red carpet—one of the samples you would get if you are out carpet shopping. Painted on it in glittering gold letters is: *Fly away with me!*

This is getting entirely out of hand and I love it.

Pre-Calc is my final class of the day and not generally full of excitement, but today I'm looking forward to it. My steps are quicker as I walk down the hall, wondering what awaits me when I step through the door.

I have no idea who delivered this one. Whoever he paid off made their exit before I got to class. The bouquet stands at least two feet tall. Set in a heavy terra-cotta pot, there are large plastic spikes jammed down into the floral foam. Attached to each spike is a bag of snack food, arranged in a semicircle fan. Alternating bags of popcorn, and Fritos. There's a card, and despite everyone in class looking at me, I can't suppress the smile that splits my face as I open it.

Looking forward to more snack adventures, it says.

Me, too, Devon. Me, too.

After school, I run to the parking lot to meet him, setting the bouquet on the ground and then throwing myself into him, pinning him to the side of his car with my kiss. We have to break it off before a teacher intervenes, since it starts getting decidedly too enthusiastic for school property.

We make the drive home laughing and snacking on Fritos. He pulls up in front of the house, and leans in to kiss me.

"You sure I can't come in and help?" he asks.

"This is my present to you," I remind him. "You've been doing stuff for me all day. It's my turn now, so no, you can't help."

"I can sit in the living room with Mojo. I won't make any noise."

I roll my eyes. "Mom is home."

"I need to meet her anyway."

"You will," I assure him with a grimace. "But let's do it later so it doesn't cast a shadow over a dinner I've slaved a few hours to make."

"You've got me terrified of her," he replies. "You know that, right?"

"She'll devour your soul, but she's going to dinner with Dad tonight, so I get you all to myself for a while. I want to keep it that way."

He lets out an exaggerated sigh. "Okay, okay. Six o'clock?"

I lean in and kiss him again. "Don't be late."

"Not by one millisecond," he promises me.

At twenty minutes to six, I'm putting the dressing on the salad and the table looks spectacular, if I do say so myself. I got the best china out of the hutch—the stuff mom only uses for Thanksgiving and Christmas. The gold damask tablecloth matches the gold chargers set under each plate. I've even got Mom's good Waterford crystal wine glasses, and the polished silver candlesticks she got as a hostess gift for some home party she threw a decade ago. There's a mulled wine scented candle on the warmer, but you can't really smell it right now over the garlic bread and chicken piccata, which is sheer perfection and very nearly done. The water for the pasta is almost boiling, my ungodly delicious tiramisu is chilling in the fridge, and I am ridiculously pleased with myself.

I set down the bottle of olive oil and balsamic vinegar salad dressing and reach for my phone as it vibrates. It's Devon.

> Hey babe
> I'm so sorry
> I have to cancel tonight

> promise I'll make it up to you
> can't get into it rn
> call you later

I stare at the phone in shock for a good thirty seconds. I reread the message. Reread it again. He's bagging out on me? On Valentine's Day? What the hell!

> what's going on?

> is everything okay?
> are you okay?

He'd *better* have a bodily injury if he's blowing me off tonight, of all nights. After all I've done here. I stare at the phone, waiting for his reply. A minute passes. Two minutes.

Screw it, I'm going to call him.

His phone rings. And rings. And rings. Voicemail. I hang up. I call again. Same thing.

I open up a FaceTime call, but it only rings and keeps ringing. I text him again.

> answer your phone

> what's going on

He doesn't answer. I sit down at the table with my head in my hand, torn between being really pissed off that he stood me up on Valentine's Day, and genuinely worried that he's hurt, or in trouble. Then I go back to pissed again because, as usual, he won't tell me a damn thing about what's really going on in his life.

I try texting him one more time, repeating my previous question, and still, no answer.

Finally, I text Jules. She doesn't have a date tonight, and she loves my chicken piccata. If she comes over and eats it, then by the time Mom and Dad get home, they'll just assume my dinner went off as planned, and Devon went home early. I won't get any questions.

And if Jules comes over, she'll keep me from walking down to Devon's house, beating on his door with my fist, and demanding that he tells me what the hell is going on.

Jules doesn't pull any punches when I open the door.

"He ghosted you on Valentine's Day?"

I opened the door wider. "Get in here," I say unceremoniously. "Eat your food."

She pushes past me, inhaling deeply and making an *mmm* sound as the smell of the garlic bread and chicken piccata fill her nostrils. She plops down at the table and start shoveling food on her plate.

"You're not eating?" She says, slurping up a long strand of spaghetti.

"Not hungry," I answer glumly. I pick up my phone, and then set it down again.

"So what's the story?" She asks through a mouthful of garlic bread. "I've seen the boy eat. What could possibly keep him from this meal?"

I shrug in what I think is a casual way, but Jules knows me too well. She gives a little head shake, like I'm a hopeless cause, and starts cutting into her chicken.

"So tell me," she says.

"There's not really anything to tell," I say. "At least nothing in the way of information. Twenty minutes before dinner he texted me to say he couldn't be here. He's been ignoring me ever since."

"Men." The anger in her voice makes me feel slightly better. Slightly.

I pull up the text and slide the phone at her. "What do you think of this?"

She reads it through and stuffs a bite of chicken into her mouth without even bothering to swallow the bite that went before it.

"Hmmm," is all she says. I don't think she can say anymore until she finishes chewing the half a chicken breast that's in her mouth. Finally, she swallows.

"Was he acting weird today?"

"No. He was perfect. The perfect boyfriend." My mouth wobbles, and I clamp my lips together. "We had such a good day."

"But he hasn't always had good days," she points at the phone with her fork. "He had that bandage on his hand. And that big old honking bruise on his forehead."

"You saw that?"

She waves her hand with a piece of garlic bread in it. "He tried to hide it under his hair, but it was big."

It *was* big. But he told me he tripped over the cat on the steps. And the hand—I don't remember what he said to explain the hand.

"Didn't Maya see him in the emergency room?" she asks. "Did you ask him about that?"

"I started to but—every time I try to talk to him about stuff that might be going on in his life, he kind of goes off on another subject."

Jules raises her eyebrows. "Well, we've ruled out the gay thing, but the dude is clearly hiding something. I mean, he's nice to everybody, and all, but you're the only one he really talks to about stuff. And nobody in the neighborhood really sees his family. They keep to themselves."

I remember the way Devon's mother looked that day when I dropped him off. No smile. Not even a wave. We'd just started dating then. But you'd think she'd at least wave to her son's girlfriend.

Then there was the night at the playground. I haven't told Jules about him crying, sitting alone on the swing in the snow. It seemed so—personal. I'm not going to tell her now, either.

"Why do you think he doesn't trust me?" I ask quietly.

"Maybe whatever's going on, he doesn't want you involved in."

"That's a bit much," I say. "He doesn't have a meth lab in the basement."

"How do you know?" Jules asks. "You haven't been to his house. And his Snap and Insta accounts only go back to December. I checked."

"I know. He told me he hates social media. He only created the accounts so he could follow me."

Jules raises her brows. "Well, that's not creepy *at all*. Has he told you why he left Florida?"

I blink at her in surprise. "I never asked. I mean, I assumed one of his parents got a job here, or something."

"Maybe they *had* to leave Florida," Jules says, biting into another slice of garlic bread.

"What—you think the state kicked them out?"

"I think maybe they wanted to start over. Maybe things weren't great in Florida. Maybe one of his parents has charges against them. Or he does. Have you Googled their names?"

"No." I open my mouth. Close it again. "I don't know his parent's names. I've never met them. He won't let me meet them yet."

"He's afraid of them," she says. "Or he's afraid of what they'll tell you about him."

My eyes narrow. "So now you think he's a criminal?"

"He could be. I mean he's been here since before Christmas, and he still hasn't tried to get a job, has he? Maybe they're afraid to let him get one."

"He's not dangerous," I snap. "I would know if he was dangerous."

"Dude—does he have a gun?" She asks in a hushed tone.

"No! Oh my God, Jules." I shake my head at her. Then I still. "I don't know. It's not something I've needed to ask him."

"Maybe you should," Jules says. "But do it in a text, just in case."

"Like I can just break that out in a conversation."

She glugs down the sparkling water I poured earlier, and puts a fist to her lips to stifle a delicate burp. Then she pushes the phone back toward me.

"You're going to have to start asking some questions," she says. "He's your boyfriend. There shouldn't be any secrets. And he's an idiot for missing out on this meal."

I stare at my phone. She's right. There shouldn't be any secrets.

We had a perfect day before the secrets unraveled it all.

I pick up the phone, and text him one more time.

> talk to me please

> I'm worried

> tell me what's going on

I wait, as Jules finishes off the last of her chicken and spaghetti, mopping up the plate with a piece of garlic bread.

Devon doesn't answer.

I PACKED UP the leftover chicken and spaghetti and gave it to Jules. There was no leftover garlic bread, and she refused the salad, so I scooped it into the trash. By the time Mom and Dad got home, the kitchen looked like no one had been there.

Like no one slaved away three hours of her life hand-breading chicken and making a lemony piccata sauce from scratch. Like no one got ghosted by the guy who was the world's greatest boyfriend earlier today.

I shut my copy of *Fahrenheit 451* with a sound of disgust. I need to finish it tonight. I should've finished it before now, because we've got a quiz tomorrow, but as usual, I procrastinated and now I'm screwed because my mind is a mess.

I throw the book onto my pillow and slide down the bed to where Mojo is laying. As I snuggle into him, he gives my cheek a lick.

"Well, at least I got kissed on Valentine's Day," I tell him as I scratch his ears. I fold them over so he looks like Princess Leia and he shakes his head to release them, then shoves his nose up into my hand, begging me for more attention.

The doorbell rings, and Mojo jumps down to scratch at the door, barking madly. I groan as I roll off the bed and let him out. I'm ready to close it again when Mom yells up to me.

"Blue! Devon is here!"

Relief floods me. Dismay follows it quickly as I realize he's down there alone with my mother. Racing down the stairs after Mojo, my stockinged feet slip on the hardwood floor at the bottom.

I skid to a stop and my relief turns to indignation as I see that he's perfectly fine. No scratches, no bruises, no broken bones.

"I was surprised you didn't stick around," my mom is saying. "I've been wanting to meet you."

"Sorry," Devon says smoothly. "Something came up, but I'm back now. I've been wanting to meet you, too."

Mom gives one of those stupid fake laughs and reaches out to put a hand on my arm.

"I was beginning to think that Blue was hiding you from me," she says with a pointed look at me.

"She didn't want to blow my cover," Devon replies, leaning in and lowering his voice. "The CIA would consider all of you collateral damage."

Mom laughs again. "He's funny," she says to me. "You didn't mention he was funny."

"You didn't tell her I was funny?" Devon says, holding a hand over his heart like he's wounded.

"It didn't come up." I really don't feel like bantering

"Why don't you come on in and we'll all chat for a bit," Mom motions toward the family room.

I ram my feet into my sneakers, which are, thank God, right next to the door.

"He can't right now," I say before Devon can get a word in. "We're going over to his house." I open the hall closet and grab my coat.

"Fifteen minutes," Mom begs. "He only just got here."

"Mom," I put a wealth of exaggeration into her name. "It's Valentine's Day. And we got interrupted. Devon forgot to bring my present—it's at his house." I shoot him a warning look.

"Yeah," he says. "Stupid me. We won't be out too late."

She lets out a sigh and finally gives up. "Home by ten-thirty," she tells me as I pull the door closed behind both of us.

Devon starts to say something but I grab his hand, pulling him down the block. I know she's probably listening at the door.

When we are far enough away from prying ears, I drop his hand and turned to face him.

"Okay, so what happened?" I demand.

He lets out a breath. "It's kind of a long story, and I don't have a lot of time right now."

"Why? Where are you going?"

"Can we go back to your house? I really don't feel like having this conversation out on the street."

I put my hands on my hips. "Why don't we go to *your* house?"

He winces. "Now is not a good time."

"Now is never a good time to go to your house. Now is never a good time to meet your parents. Now is never a good time to ask you anything about your past." I say, waving my arms. "Why is that?"

"Look, I know there's a lot I haven't told you. And I'm sorry—"

"So sorry that you ditched me on Valentine's Day?"

"Bad timing," he says, wincing again. "I'm really sorry. I told you I was sorry. I texted you as soon as I could." His eyes brighten. "Is there any food left over?"

I stare at him incredulously. "That's all you care about? The food?"

"No, of course not."

"I'm trying to have a conversation. Why did you move here?"

He looks taken aback. "What?"

"You heard me. I'm asking about your life. About your life before you came here because apparently you don't have one. Why is that?"

"I told you, I lived in Florida," he says defensively.

"Yeah, and that's pretty much all you've told me," I fume. "I'm your girlfriend, and I can't really tell anyone anything about you. You've got no past anyone can turn up. Nothing on social media. Google has some scores from a few golf tournaments at your old school but that's about it."

His eyes go wide and he freezes. "What—you're running a background check on me?"

"Do I need to?" I demand.

"What is that supposed to mean?"

"You tell me. You're the one with all the secrets. Beaten up hands, bruises on your body, weeks out of school, ambulance rides to the emergency room." I tick them off on my fingers as I list them. "Am I missing anything?"

"Yes, as a matter of fact you are," he spits out. "Apparently you're missing the part where I'm your boyfriend and we care about each other. You'd rather dig through my past and make up your own stories."

"What the hell else am I supposed to do? I ask you about stuff and you change the subject."

His jaw tightens. "I know I haven't handled this right—"

"No, you haven't. I've got enough shit to deal with at school without people asking if you're going to come to school with an assault rifle or something."

"You honestly think I would—" His mouth opens. Closes. Opens again. "So you've got the school gossiping about me?"

I poke a finger in the middle of his chest. "Don't put this on me. We've been dating for weeks, and you won't let me into your life. I can't trust somebody who's keeping secrets from me. For all I know, you've got another girl on the side. Maybe back in Florida."

"I told you I didn't. And why did your mom think I'd eaten dinner with you?" He accuses. "Who were you cooking for? Did you text one of your *whatevers* and let them know there was an open spot?"

"Maybe I did!"

He turns abruptly on his heel. "I'm done."

I grab his arm. "Well, I'm not. If we're going to make a relationship work, you can't be closing up on me, and ghosting me when I'm trying to find out what the hell is going on. And then you show up here tonight and all I can think is, 'Somebody had better be dead' and you look fine. You're joking with my mother. You're asking me about leftovers. What am I supposed to think?"

He goes utterly still. His mouth tightens into a thin line and he shakes his head.

"I have to go," is all he says.

I watch him walk away, because I don't know what else to do. And somehow, I make it up the stairs into my room and lock the door before I shove my face into my pillow and cry.

DEVON WASN'T IN school today. I spent a miserable night tossing and turning, replaying our conversation in my head.

I shouldn't have jumped on him like that. I should have given him a chance to explain.

I did give him a chance to explain. He told me he didn't have time to explain and he asked about leftover chicken.

I'm really, really mad at him.

I really, really miss him.

I shouldn't have been so harsh.

I let him walk all over me.

Back and forth, back and forth. I feel ripped apart. Everything was so good. It was so, so good. Why didn't I just leave things like they were?

Because he doesn't trust you, a small voice whispers from the back of my mind. I wish I could dig that voice out with a fork, but it would still be there. And every day that we're together it will get louder, so last night's conversation was bound to happen sooner or later. I just wish it had been later.

I keep looking at my phone to see if he's texted me and I somehow missed it—which is not possible because I'm checking my phone constantly, and pretty much kept it in my hand all day.

If I don't hear from him by the time school is over, I'm going to text him. Or maybe not. I don't know what I'm going to say, but I've got to say something. But he should text me first. After all, he's the one who walked away.

Did he really think I called Austin and invited him to Valentine's Day dinner after the way he's treated me? Just because I was mad at my boyfriend?

I shift back from sad to pissed off again, and then I remember that I'd hinted Devon was a potential mass murderer, so I guess we are more than even when it comes to jumping to conclusions.

Not that I really feel that way about him. I was just angry and it came out. Despite what Jules says, I can't feel like Devon is dangerous to me. Whatever it is he's hiding, it was in the past. I'm pretty sure. Or it's nothing like that. I believe that.

I have to believe that.

I left before Mom got up this morning just in case she wanted to ask me why I ran back into the house ten minutes after I'd walked out last night. Why I pounded up the stairs and slammed the door to my room and locked it. Hopefully, she didn't hear me crying, but this is Mom. She hears everything.

I work after school, and I'm three hours into my shift before I get a break. BurgerMania has outdoor seating, but not a lot of people use it in February in Pennsylvania. It's a good place to check your phone, though, if you're likely to burst into tears as you read your text messages.

Or your lack of text messages.

I've decided against texting Devon. But I can't leave things like they were. I posted a selfie last night where I looked kind of thoughtful and a little sad. I captioned it: *late night thoughts*.

Okay, maybe I looked a lot sad. He had to have seen that I looked sad.

But he didn't comment. And he didn't text.

I think about driving to his house after work today, but the mental image of me standing on his front porch sobbing is a real deterrent.

I put my forehead down on the cold, metal table, and will myself not to cry. I've only got ten minutes of break left, so I need to keep it together.

A hand prods my shoulder, and I let out a startled squeak.

"You okay?"

Maya is standing there staring down at me.

"What—what are you doing here?" I sound really stupid—like I'm accusing her of a crime or something. "Sorry," I mumble. "Bad day."

"I was going through the drive-thru and saw you back here. I wanted to talk to you, anyway." She slides onto the bench across from me. "You look rough."

"I'm sure it's all over school," I say. "About me and Devon."

She looks confused. "What? Did you break up? After all that stuff he did on Valentine's Day?"

Well, what do you know? Jules kept her mouth shut. Maybe she's not such a bad friend after all.

"No, not really. Maybe." My eyes fill with tears. "I'm not sure where we're at right now."

"That sucks." She flexes her hand.

"How's it feeling?" I ask. "What did your mom say?"

"I told her I missed a rebound and ended up going into the wall at basketball practice. She believed it."

"Does it still hurt?"

"A little. It's just stiff." She flexes her fingers again. "Listen—about the other day—"

I hold up a hand to head her off. "It's okay," I say.

"Did I hurt your car?"

"No. I guess your hand is softer."

"Guess it is." She stretches her fingers one more time.

"What did you need to talk to me about?"

She looks around, but nobody's listening in. There aren't even any cars in the drive-thru right now.

"Please don't tell anyone what I told you," she pleads.

"I didn't. I wouldn't." I look around, too, for some reason. "That was really personal and I know you didn't mean to share it with me."

"Thanks." She starts to get up.

"Maya, I've been thinking. About your dad."

She eyes me warily and sits back down. "What?"

"I know what he did—with the texts and all—I know that's hard. Coming on top of losing him that had to be really, really hard."

"The last picture I have of us is from my birthday," she tells me. "I see that picture and I think, 'Look at that girl. Right now she has no idea her dad is a lying piece of shit whose selfishness is going to drop a bomb in her life and wreck her mother.' But my right now and her right now are different. Her right now was great. She was happy. Her dad loved her and loved her mom and it was all good. I can't have that in *my* right now."

That horrible, clawing guilt is shredding my insides again.

"I have absolutely no right to tell you how to feel about any of that," I admit. "But Maya, he's still who he was to you. He's still the father that you knew—and loved. He just made a mistake."

"Yeah, I know." Her voice is soft, but she doesn't sound pissed at me so I go on.

"He didn't do any of that to hurt you. He loved you, Maya. None of that's changed. I don't know how things were between him and your mother, but none of that had anything to do with his feelings for you. You should forgive him, if you can. He was human. And humans make mistakes."

She swallows hard. "I know."

"And for what it's worth, I'm sorry things are hard for you at home—knowing what you know. And with you helping your mother and sisters. You shouldn't have to deal with all that. The worst thing you should have to deal with in high school is Austin Bradley."

She gives an awkward laugh. "He was a pretty miserable experience."

"The worst," I agree.

Now it's her turn to look guilty. "Sorry I tried to use him to get at you."

I give her a dismissive wave. "You did me a favor."

She did. She really did. Even if Devon and I are through—the thought makes my throat close up—but even if we are, Austin was no good for me. Or for Maya, apparently.

"You're welcome," she says.

"Now if we can just get the stupid club figured out, maybe we can both have a better life."

Well, maybe one of us can, anyway.

"We should do your idea," she says. "The spa thing."

"You think?"

"It's easiest." She pushes up to her feet.

"Yeah, it is. I should get back inside. See ya."

"Later."

I stand up and stomp some feeling back into my feet. Then I pick up my phone and check my texts one more time before I go back inside.

And even though Hank put me on fryers tonight, the heat and steam can't seem to touch all the cold that's inside me.

"SO WE'VE DECIDED on the spa idea?" Mrs. Ramsey glances at the paper I hand her. "You both agree on this?"

Maya nods. "It's going to be more than beauty, though. We can talk about dealing with stress and relaxation techniques, too. You can probably help us with that."

"I'd be happy to assist," Mrs. Ramsey says. "What else are you going to add in?"

"My mom has some yoga DVDs that she doesn't use anymore," I suggest. 'Fifteen Minute Yoga' is actually one of them. It has a bunch of mini yoga sessions that might be good to try."

"You'd have to get permission to use the gym," Mrs. Ramsey says. "You can't do yoga on a hard floor, and you can't assume every student will have their own yoga mat."

I make a face and catch Maya doing the same thing. All of this is so complicated. Everything we suggest comes with three other things we have to do to support it.

"I can talk to Mrs. Fleenor," Maya says, mentioning the gym teacher who's also the basketball coach. "And we have some other ideas that we still need to bounce off of each other."

Mrs. Ramsey sits back at her desk and folds her arms, studying us. "Well, girls, I have to say, it does seem like you're working together better. There hasn't been a single raised voice or dirty look since you got here."

"We just want to get this done," Maya says.

"Yeah, we both have better places to be," I agree.

"And that's something I can get behind," Mrs. Ramsey says. "I can think of a dozen other things I could spend my afternoon doing, as well. So let's get this club launched."

She gestures to us as we both murmur an agreement.

Maya's hand still looks pretty bruised, so I grab my chair and drag it over next to her.

"I can do the writing," I say.

"Thanks," she replies, and out of the corner of my eye I see Mrs. Ramsey smile. That's probably the first time she's ever heard that word while we've been meeting.

I pull a notebook and pen out of my backpack and set them down on the desk in front of me. We start working through suggestions, beginning with yoga, adding in a spa day where we try out skincare or aromatherapy products, then we put in a section on healthy eating, battling insomnia, and stretches that can be done while sitting in a desk.

We've actually got a pretty good-sized list going, and it's not as hard as I thought to come up with things. Maya suggests we do an afternoon tea, featuring soothing teas like chamomile and green tea blends. Good God, have I got chamomile for her. Then again, her family owns a coffee shop. She may have more chamomile than I do. Either way, we are equipped for that and it sounds kind of fun. We are working together pretty well for the first half-hour, when Mrs. Ramsey clears her throat.

"Girls, I need to run to the office for a few minutes," she says, leafing through the stack of papers on her desk again and pulling out a couple of sheets. "You two keep on working, and when I get back we'll go over some of the things you've written down, and discuss possible faculty sponsors."

As soon as the door closes behind her, I lean back in my seat.

"Well, at least we have her approval," I say. "This whole ordeal should be over with soon."

"Yeah," Maya agrees. She points at the notebook. "It's actually not a bad idea, you know. The kind of club I wouldn't mind joining."

"I know, right?"

"I mean, if I had the time."

"Yeah, who has the time?" I say. "Which is why we're all so stressed."

"Truth."

I pick up my phone, check it, put it back.

"He's still not talking to you?" Maya asks.

"He's been out sick," I say defensively. "He's got a lot going on."

"Don't we all." She glances over at the door, checking it. "Hey, what you said yesterday—about my dad. Thanks again. It helped."

"I'm glad. I know I'm the last person who should be giving you any kind of advice in this situation," I say. "But I know how things are with me and my father. I feel like I barely know my dad. If you're lucky enough to have a father who loved you, then that's what you should remember."

Her eyes lock on mine. "So change it."

"What? My dad?"

"You've still got him. He's still here. If you feel like you barely know him, you should try to change that."

"He's so busy," I say. "And I don't even know what we'd talk about, anyway."

"You should try, though," she says. "If I still had my father—" her voice breaks. "I'm just saying, I would be talking to him. I would be trying to stay close. The longer you let things go on like this, I think the easier it'll be for you to not connect—know what I mean?"

"Yeah, I do. It's just—we're all so busy."

"Make the time. Get them to make the time. You only get so much of it."

"I know. But my mom and dad—it's hard to talk to them. First they were pissed at me about Jack, and now they're pissed me about all this stuff going on between us—"

She turns to face me. "Why are they pissed at you for Jack?" She demands. "Like any of that is your fault."

The irony of that remark doesn't go by me, but I'm not going to bring that up right now.

"They're pissed because I haven't gone to see him since he started serving his time. I just—I don't know what to say to him. I don't know how to face him. I'm so angry at him." I turn pleading eyes to her. "Maya, I don't know if he really was at fault—he might've been. And if he was—how could he? How could he do that to you, to your family? To himself? And then all the stuff my parents had to go through."

"And everything you had to go through," Maya says. "Facing me."

I nod. "It's like a hurricane that just slammed through so many lives, all because of that night. I don't know what really happened—and honestly, I'm not sure Jack knows, either."

She plays with the string on her hoodie, and takes a long moment before finding the words she needs.

"Maybe we'll never really know the truth," she finally says. "We can all kind of write our own story based on everything that happened, but who knows? Who really knows?"

"I'm sorry," I say to her. I feel like I need to. Like I can't say it enough.

"None of this is easy for anybody," Maya says. "But what you said about forgiveness—" She takes in a deep breath. "It goes for your brother, too."

My eyes go wide. "You forgive Jack?"

"No," she says quietly—and firmly. "I'm not there yet. I'm not sure if I ever will be. But I'm not his sister."

I look away, and force the words out of my very tight throat. "Yeah, I guess." The irony grates on me again and this time I have to remark. "You're telling me to forgive my brother but you were screaming at me a few weeks ago for hugging him in the courtroom."

"I know. I was pissed. Pissed is easier to manage than sad."

Tell me about it.

Her hand reaches out, touches my arm. "Listen, you're not the only one who's been thinking about stuff. What would I do if that was one of my sisters? Someday they're going to be driving, and going to parties. What if something like this happened to one of them? All it would take is one minute of bad judgment. What would I do? Defend them?"

"It's hard to defend."

"Yeah," she agrees. "But I'd still want to help them. And if people were talking about them, I'd want them to shut up. My mom—and my dad—they'd do whatever they had to do to help them. If we had the money to hire the best lawyer, if we had other ways they could try to make it easier for them—they would do it. Just like yours did."

"I guess."

"They would. And I'd want them to."

I stay silent. I'm not going to point out that it would have been great if she'd tried that line of thinking before we got roped into starting a club.

"I'm just saying—he's your only brother. And just like your parents, the space between you is a choice. You should at least try. Because someday there might be space between you that's permanent. And you'll wish for every moment back so you could redo it."

Her eyes well with tears and so do mine. I reach in my backpack to pull out my packet of tissues.

"There's two left," I say, handing one over to her. She dabs at her eyes, and laughs.

"You need to get me one of these goodie bags," she says. "Oh, and by the way, the party was terrific. My sister's friends all loved their bags."

"I'm sorry again—about the business card."

She waves the tissue at me in dismissal. "They're over it. My mom felt really guilty for yelling at them, so she took them on a shopping spree at the mall."

"I'm glad it worked out for them."

"You took a big chance by offering to help me," she goes on. "Right now, let me help you. Talk to your family. Seriously."

"Maybe we should add family counseling into our club," I say. "You're pretty good at it."

"So are you," Maya says. "And you think we're the only ones with family trouble? Girl, I could write a book about some of the kids in this school."

"Truth. Some of them are a hot mess."

"They need more help than us."

"Right now," I agree, "they need our club more than we do."

Mrs. Ramsey breezes back in, carrying three cans of Diet Coke. She sets a can in front of each of us.

"How's it going?" She asks. "Have you got everything figured out?"

Maya and I have been staring at each other since Mrs. Ramsey walked in, as if we're both stuck on the same idea.

"I think we've got a few more things to add," I say.

THEY TAKE MY driver's license at the desk, checking my name against the list of pre-approved visitors. Then I follow my parents through the steel doors, after the guard buzzes us through.

The hallway smells like sweat and disinfectant. There are two guys mopping at the end of the hall, but we turn before we reach them, into a large open room. A cafeteria, from the look of the tables. The room reeks of garlic.

There are already a few dozen inmates scattered around the tables with their family members, or friends. Some are playing board games, and one guy looks like he's opening presents. It must be his birthday.

What a rotten place to spend a birthday.

Jack's birthday is coming up in two months, so that's going to be him. Opening presents on a cafeteria table in a place that smells like disinfectant, sweat, and garlic.

Finally, I see him. He's wearing a gray cotton shirt and pants that look like the scrubs a doctor or nurse would wear. Which is kind of ironic, because Jack wants to study medicine when he goes to college. I wonder if he still does? Did the accident make him re-evaluate that? If he's in a hospital emergency room, will it trigger bad memories?

I never thought to wonder before, but it's entirely possible he has some PTSD from this. Jules's mom was in an accident a few years back that totaled her car and gave her a concussion and a broken arm. She's still sort-of afraid to drive. Every time we're in the car with her and she has to merge into traffic, she hyperventilates. Jules and I used to think it was funny.

It's not funny, really.

Jack stands up as he sees us approaching. He's not surprised to see me because he had to tell them I was visiting so I could be on the list—but he does look glad. His smile is wide, and genuine. And right now, I'm smiling back just as wide. So wide, my face hurts.

He hugs Mom first, and she smothers him with it, rocking him back and forth so long it's got to be embarrassing for him. Dad hugs him next, and I wonder when Dad hugged him last, before all of this came down.

Then Jack steps forward and his arms surround me, and I'm clinging to him.

"I'm sorry," I whisper.

"S'alright," he mumbles, giving me a squeeze. He pulls back, and holds me at arm's length. "I'm glad you came."

"I came for the garlic," I tell him.

"No vampires in this group," Dad quips.

"They made lasagna for lunch," Jack says, scrunching up his face. "There's like, a gallon of grease floating on the top of each pan."

Mom looks nauseated. "I hate that they feed you that kind of stuff," she says. "We'll just have to go out and bring some lunch back."

"Chinese?" Jack asks, hopefully.

"We had Chinese last time," Mom says.

"I like Chinese," he counters.

"He likes Chinese," Dad says. "And so do I." He looks at me, and I nod. "And so does Blue."

Mom gives up, realizing she is outnumbered. Jack motions us over to one of the tables, and we take a seat, with Mom commandeering the spot next to Jack. Dad and I slide in on the opposite side, and for a moment we all sit staring at each other.

"So, what's new?" I ask, before it gets more awkward.

Jack waves a hand over his shoulder. "Same old stuff. Nothing changes around here. They're big on routine."

"Are you still doing laundry?" I ask.

"Yeah, but they're moving me to maintenance week-after-next."

"So you get to fix stuff?"

"I get to change light bulbs. And paint." He shrugs. "It could be worse."

Yes, it could be worse. It could all be a lot worse. This place isn't any place I'd want to be, and it isn't any place I want my brother to be. But it's better than being in a federal prison on a manslaughter charge, and it's better than dead. He's got a little less than four months, and then he can return to his life, whatever that works out to be now.

"Aiden and Nick told me to tell you hi," Mom says. "I saw them the other day when I was making a delivery to Nick's mom. Nick says he's switching to Penn State."

"That's good," Jack says, but the smile that he forces looks more like a grimace. All of his friends are a year ahead of him in college now. They won't be graduating together because he was dealing with the trial and then doing this.

Dad sets the bag full of stuff that we brought on the table. The guards already looked through it all when we first got here. It's just antiperspirant, toothpaste and shampoo. I tried to load up the snack food in there, but Mom says it's against the rules. If he wants snack food, he has to eat it during the visit or to buy it from the commissary—he's not allowed to store it in his room.

"We added money into your commissary account," Dad says, as if he's riding my train of thought.

"Thanks," Jack says. He looks at me. "How's school?"

How's Maya? He's really asking.

"It's going okay," I say. "Better."

"That's good."

"Hank says he's putting you on the schedule the minute you get back," I tell him.

"He's only going to have me for the summer," he reminds me. "I'm up to Boston in August."

"He doesn't care. He's having a hard time finding anybody since Eric quit."

"Eric quit? What happened?"

"He got a job at Target. They pay more."

"Everybody pays more than Hank," Jack says with a look of pure disgust.

"You should work at Target," Mom says to me. "Think of the employee discount. And you wouldn't come home smelling like red meat."

"She'd make you shop for her with your employee discount," Dad points out, and quite accurately.

I look around the room. "So that's all they have you do with your time, laundry and painting?"

"It's a boot camp program, remember?" He tells me. "Since they can't train us to fight and use weapons, we get all the physical stuff like calisthenics at six a.m. and a ten mile runs, and then they fill up most of the rest of the time with all the grunt work it takes to keep this place running. The group sessions and classes are a joke."

Mom's eyes narrow. "You need to be taking this seriously, Jack. You were very lucky to get in here, and we want this time to go by without any issues."

"I'm just saying that group therapy with a bunch of guys who sold drugs or broke into houses isn't really teaching me anything," he says.

"I would hope it's teaching you that you don't want to be here again," Dad notes.

Jack nods begrudgingly. "And we have these 'Betterment' classes three days a week," he goes on. "Mostly it's just motivational stuff that sounds like Mom's Post-it notes. And we talk about career plans."

"Well, at least that's easy for you," Mom says brightly. "With your scholarships, you're all set."

He rolls his eyes. "Nobody knows about that. Can you just keep your voice down please?"

"What?" Mom looks offended. "You should be proud of that."

"I'll sound like just another bored rich kid, who got in trouble because he's an asshole," he says, making a face. "Some of these kids have real problems. I just let them talk."

"And you don't have problems?" Mom asks.

"Leave him alone." Mom's head swivels to look at me, clearly annoyed that I interrupted. "You don't know who he has to deal with in this place," I tell her. "Or what people are saying behind his back. Or how he feels when they're looking at him."

My eyes meet Jack's, and he gives me a grateful nod.

Dad clears his throat. "Well," he says. "If we're going to go get Chinese, we'd better get a move on."

Mom sighs. "All right. You want your usual?" she asks Jack.

"Make it sesame chicken this time," he tells her.

"I'll have chicken and broccoli, sauce on the side," she tells Dad.

"Why don't you come with me?" he replies. "That's a lot of food to juggle. I'll need an extra hand."

She wants to object, but Dad sends her another message through his eyes, which shift from me to Jack, then back to her again.

"Okay, okay," she finally relents. "Blue? Shrimp fried rice?"

"And two spring rolls," I add. "And a Diet Coke."

"You really should drink water," she says.

"Diet Coke it is, and iced tea for Jack," Dad says, getting to his feet. "Maybe when we get back we can all play a board game." He gestures toward a family playing Monopoly at one of the other tables.

"Board games here are crap," Jack says. "Monopoly has half its money missing. And somebody wrote all over the Scrabble tiles with a Sharpie."

"Do they have Uno?" I ask.

"Used to," he replies. "Until the deck got down to like, twelve cards."

"We'll bring a fresh deck next time," Dad promises. He takes Mom by the elbow and leads her out the door.

Jack's shoulders slump in relief as soon as they're gone.

"Is it always like that?" I ask. "Do they bust on you every visit?"

"Not every time," he says tiredly. "To tell you the truth, I like that better than when she used to cry. She cried a lot the first few visits."

"I'm surprised she hasn't tried to get you to recruit people for her downline."

He smiles. "She did. One of the girls in the office gets regular deliveries." He glances around at the cafeteria. "Want to get out of here?"

My eyes go wide. "You want me to break you out?"

He leans over and lightly smacks my arm. "No, you big derp. I was talking about the exercise yard. It's better than sitting in here. I'm tired of smelling garlic."

"It'd be nice to stretch my legs after that car ride."

"Did you fake sleep all the way up here so they'd leave you alone?" Jack walks over to get his coat and let the guard know where we're going.

"Who's faking?" I answer. "I'll sleep wherever I can."

He directs me through another set of doors and then outside into a large open area surrounded by a chain-link fence topped with barbed wire. It's easily the size of a football field, circled by a track worn into the grass. At the far end, there's an area that looks like an obstacle course, with tires laid out on the ground, overhead bars to cross, and a couple of walls with ropes attached at the top.

I gesture toward a pile of sandbags stacked against one of the walls.

"Is that to help you get over the wall?" I ask as we begin walking.

"Nope. That's what the ropes are for," he replies. "The sandbags we have to pick up and carry and then stack somewhere else. And then pick them up and carry and stack them back again."

"Seriously?" I sneer.

He holds up an arm and curls it to show off his bicep. "I'm starting to look ripped. You should see my abs. One hundred sit-ups every morning."

"You really have calisthenics at six a.m.?" I ask. "In the freezing cold?"

"Yeah, it sucks balls."

"It does."

Suddenly, my miserable semester doesn't seem nearly as bad in comparison. I get to wake up in a cushy bed in my room, in a house that smells like Mom's Solstice Sparkle scented wax melts. I can sleep in on weekends. And since I don't have gym this semester, my physical activity is entirely voluntary and most definitely does *not* include calisthenics. I know Jack is shrugging it off, but damn. It does suck balls.

"This whole place is awful," I tell him honestly.

"The group sessions are a waste," he goes on. "Everybody says the same old shit in response to their stupid questions. But the individual counseling helps." He takes a breath. "It helps a lot."

"I guess nobody thinks to ask how you're dealing with the hardest part of this."

Silence hangs between us. Finally, Jack shrugs like it's no big deal, but his eyes show it is. And I know it is.

"You know Dad—if we all just ignore it, it'll go away. Mom keeps telling me to be resilient. Keep climbing until I'm on top again. Pave a new road. Bullshit like that. And you don't talk to me at all."

"I'm sorry. And I'm sorry you have to be here." My voice is a strangled thing, like the guilt is lodged in my throat.

"You're not the one who put me here," he reminds me.

I stop walking. "Hey," I say. "Can I ask you something?"

He stops, too, at the seriousness on my face. "Sure."

"That night..." I don't have to clarify which night I'm talking about. He watches me in wary silence as I fight to ask the question I'm not sure I want the answer to.

"That night," I say again. "When you texted me. And called me." I take in a deep breath and let it out. The words come out in a rush. "Were you trying to call me to come and get you? Were you afraid to drive?"

He looks confused. His eyes narrow and then shift up and off to the side as if he's trying to remember.

"I called you?" He asks, still confused.

"You texted me first, and when I didn't answer you tried to call me—about an hour before the accident. But I was asleep. I'm sorry I didn't answer you. I was asleep." I hold my hands out in a pleading gesture. "I'm sorry."

"Shit." He reaches out, grabs my hands. "Blue—"

He shakes his head. "I don't even remember. Maybe I was—wait—I was trying to remember the name of that kid who lived in the neighborhood that ate the stick. Remember? We dared him?"

"Conner Bateman?" I ask, screwing up my face. "Why would you call me about Conner Bateman?"

"There was a guy at that party who looked just like him," he runs his hand through his hair. "Or what I thought he would have grown up to look like. He was from Downingtown."

"Didn't Conner's family move to New Jersey?"

"I thought so, but this kid looked a lot like him. They could've been twins." He looks at me again. "You thought I was trying to call you because I was too drunk to drive?"

I shrug, and my eyes fill up. "I don't know."

"I didn't feel that drunk," he says quietly. "I didn't feel drunk at all that night. Seriously. I mean, I had a couple of beers, but it had been over an hour since the last one by the time I left. You know I wouldn't have gotten in the car if I thought I was drunk."

"I didn't think you would," I said.

"I know I was close to the limit when they gave me the blood test, but I didn't feel drunk," he says again. He's silent for a minute, and his mouth goes tight, as if there are more words, but he's not sure he wants to say them.

"I guess I could have been too buzzed to really judge my limit," he admits. "I just don't know."

He shoves his hands in his coat pockets and starts walking, so I fall into step beside him. "I've gone over that night so many times," he says. "It all happened so fast, and some of it's such a blur because of the concussion."

"I know."

"I wish I could take it back. I wish I could go back in time, and never go to that party. If I hadn't been on that road, everything would be different now. Everything."

He walks faster because he doesn't want me to see him rubbing his eyes. Up until the accident, I hadn't seen him cry since he was six and he jumped off the monkey bars on the playground and broke his wrist.

"I'm sorry," I say again. "I wish I knew how to make it all better. For everybody."

He looks at me and his face softens. "Is she still giving you a hard time? Maya?"

"Not really," I say. "Not anymore. Believe it or not, we've been talking."

He looks surprised. "You're friends now?"

"Not exactly," I say. "They made us do detention. We have to develop a club together."

He makes a face. "What's the point in that?"

"Teaching us to get along," I say with an eyeroll.

"That's stupid."

"Yeah."

"I guess it worked for you. You said you two are cool now."

"I don't know what we are. But we're not fighting anymore."

"That's good. That's good." His relief is apparent. Was he really that worried about me? I feel a twinge of guilt again. I haven't been nearly as worried about him, and he's the one dealing with all of . . . this.

"Does anybody in school ask about me?" He wants to know. "Are they talking about me?"

"No, not really," I tell him honestly.

"I don't know if that makes me feel better, or worse."

"It would've been that way if you were in college right now," I tell him. "You know how high school kids are. It's all about the drama. You're not drama anymore. Despite everything that's happened, you're old news."

"I guess." He shrugs. "Maybe I should have eaten a stick so people would remember me."

"Mom would be thrilled that you're getting fiber in your diet."

He huffs a laugh and we stand silently, watching our breath curl in the air.

"Don't let her get you down," he says. "She means well. And honestly, sometimes I miss her when I'm here. I miss all of you."

"I miss you, too. And I'm sorry I haven't come before now. Or called you. Or written you back. Not that I would ever write a letter."

"It's okay," he says. "You came today."

"I'll come next time, too. We'll play Uno."

He tries to smile, and I know the memory of our family Uno games is making him sad as much as happy. Me, too. We haven't done that sort of stuff in a long time. Once we got older—and Jack started high school hockey, and then I started high school, and we both got jobs—along with Dad's job and Mom's down-line, we're just too busy for stuff. Family stuff.

"We should get back," Jack finally says. "It's freezing out here. And Mom will be sneaking broccoli into my sesame chicken if I don't grab it away from her first."

We pick up our pace, and circle back toward the doors.

"Hey, didn't you have Mrs. Linza?" I ask him.

"Yeah. You have her for English?"

"I have to do a presentation. The *Fahrenheit 451* thing."

"We read *1984*."

"Of course you did," I grumble. "I have to pick a book that I would preserve for all posterity. Any ideas? Do you have any good books in your room?"

"Do *not* be nosing around in my room," he warns me. "Just pick an easy book. Make it a short one."

"I grabbed some dumb book of Mom's."

He shakes his head. "It should at least be a book you like. Linza will be able to tell if you're just faking through the presentation."

"Yeah, I guess."

As we make the final turn back toward the building, we see Mom and Dad pull into the parking lot. She waves at us as they're getting out of the car.

"Race you inside," Jack challenges.

"Not fair!" I exclaim as he takes off in a burst of speed and I run to catch up. "I'm not working out every morning. I'm out of shape."

"Later, Barfinator," he calls over his shoulder.

For a moment, he's eight, and I'm six, and we are on the playground at school, or in the neighborhood. And he's running and I'm running, and we're both laughing. And in a minute we're going to go inside and eat Chinese food, and we'll almost feel like a family.

Almost.

Mostly.

It's not perfect. But we're all here. We're all here for each other.

Despite the sweat, disinfectant, and garlic—it's not the absolute worst place to be.

IN THE CAR, I try to get some work done on my book presentation. We've got a two hour ride home, so I might as well make good use of it.

Except my traitorous brain keeps making me check my phone over and over. Still no texts. It's been three days, and Devon hasn't been in school.

I finally broke down and texted him last night. If I thought this was all because we had a fight, I would've left him alone. But he's missed school. Something is wrong. Something is really wrong.

All I said was *I'm here if you want to talk*. I left the door open. The rest is up to him.

I've had a lot of time to think since my last conversation with Maya—about my parents, about Jack—and about Devon. Perspective is an important thing. How things are right now doesn't have to be the way things are forever. Not with Maya, not with my family, and not with Devon.

So much about Devon and me was right. We laughed. A lot. We talked—really talked—about so much stuff. All kinds of things. One night we went to the playground and laid on the picnic table and stared up at the stars. It was freezing cold but the night was crystal clear and we talked about solar systems and extraterrestrials and climate change and the real meaning of life. The next day at lunch we had an entire conversation about paper cuts and the ways they could legitimately be used as a form of torture during wartime.

Then there's all the dozens of little, intimate things, things Devon always did that made me feel... cherished. The way he used to play with my hair when we were sitting next to each other. He'd put his arm around me and his fingers would just idly play with the ends of my hair. He loved it when it started to frizz up. He liked my curls. And when we'd say goodnight in person before he'd leave to go home, he'd always kiss my forehead after he kissed my lips. Just one soft little kiss and he'd say "sweet dreams." If we were saying good night on FaceTime, he'd make me hold the phone to my forehead so he could kiss it.

Before Devon, I would have rolled my eyes if a girl told me her boyfriend did that. But Devon changed me. He made me notice all the little things and not just brush them away and consider them stupid and oh my God, do I miss him. I miss him so much.

I miss my boyfriend, but more than anything I miss my friend.

Maybe I'm giving myself way more credit in his thoughts than I actually deserve. Whatever is going on in his life, he doesn't want me to be part of it. And after what I said to him, I probably don't deserve to be a part of his life at all.

I can't keep thinking about this, or I'll open the car door and just jump out. Okay, that's dramatic, and I wouldn't do it. But I can't keep thinking about him. About us.

Enough. I need to concentrate on my homework. I skim through *Mindfulness Over Matter* yet again and it's just so boring.

I wonder what Mrs. Linza would do if my presentation featured *Pirate Rogue and the Seas of Time*. I'm sure the class will understand the need to preserve a story about a time traveling pirate and the deadly female assassin who was sent to kill him but instead falls in love with him. He does spend half the novel shirtless. Mrs. Linza should appreciate that, at the very least.

I slam my notebook shut with a disgusted sound. This whole project is useless.

"What are you working on?" Mom asks over her shoulder from the front seat.

"This stupid project for English Lit. We had to read *Fahrenheit 451*—"

"Great book!" Dad interrupts.

"You read it?" The only thing I ever see my dad reading are his business books, and stuff on his computer. He actually reads for pleasure?

"It was a long time ago," he says. "But I loved reading all of Ray Bradbury's stuff. Just about any Sci-Fi, really."

My dad likes Sci-Fi? Bizarre.

"You know how in the story, the new government is burning all the books and everybody picks one book to memorize so it can be preserved?" I ask. "Mrs. Linza wants us each to pick a book and give a presentation about what we love about the book and why we think it needs to be passed down."

"What's your book?" Mom asks.

"I haven't picked one yet. I mean, I sort of grabbed one of your books thinking I could make it work, but—"

"Really?" She looks surprised. "Which one?"

"*Mindfulness Over Madness*," I reply. "I thought I could get something out of it, but it's just not working for me."

She makes a face. "Yeah, that one's pretty dry."

"I thought you liked all that motivational stuff."

"I try to keep myself inspired," she says. "But some of these women—" She makes the face again. "They're just so preachy and full of themselves. You don't have a book of your own that you like?"

"Nothing I want to share with the class," I say. "Do you have any other books you can recommend?"

What the hell, it's worth a try.

"You could do an old classical book," Mom says. "Teachers always love it when you choose a classic."

"Any one in particular?" I ask.

She purses her lips, considering. "Something from Jane Astin?"

"Austin. Her books are long. This thing is due on Tuesday."

"And you're just now starting on it?" Dad admonishes.

"I've got enough put together about Mom's book that I can finish up if I want to. I just don't want to do that book. But I don't want to do any of this stupid project."

"Hmm," Dad says thoughtfully. "How about Aldous Huxley's Brave New World? Or maybe George Orwell?"

I wave a hand. "Overdone."

"Well, I'd suggest something I've enjoyed reading," Mom says, "but it's all self-help and the occasional romance. What about those books with the vampires and werewolves? God, I loved those."

My jaw drops. "You're a *Twilight* fan?"

"Every single time you and Jack went down for a nap, I was buried in those books. Couldn't get enough of them." She sighs.

I have to ask. "Team Edward or Team Jacob?"

"Team hot wolf boy any day of the week," she says, and I feel myself inwardly cringe.

"Yeah, I got the benefit of her reading those books, too," Dad says, waggling his eyebrows and reaching over to squeeze her knee.

I'm now cringing so hard I think my body is going to invert completely. This is not the direction I intended for this conversation.

"Of course," Mom says, "I wasn't reading those books to *you* back then. Maybe you could do your book report on *Goodnight Moon*. You loved that one!"

I smile at the memory. "Yeah, I did."

"It's very soothing. You wanted it every night. Or maybe that funny book with the sheep."

"Ugh, the sheep book," Dad interjects.

"You were stuck on that one for a while before you fell in love with *Goodnight Moon*," Mom says.

"I'm not doing my presentation on *Moo Baa LaLaLa*." I reply. "I guess I'll just stick with what I've got."

"I was a big fan of *Everyone Poops*," Dad says.

"I'm not doing that one, either."

"That's a great book to preserve for all posterity," Mom says with a laugh. I picture Mrs. Linza's face as I walk the class through *Everyone Poops*, and I laugh too.

"You could bring in some visual aids," Dad suggests, and we all laugh harder. God, when was the last time we all laughed together?

"Hey," I say. "When Jack mentioned Uno, I was thinking—we should try to do some stuff together sometime—the three of us. Uno isn't as much fun with just three people but, maybe we could go to a movie or something?"

My mother looks at me for a solid five seconds with her mouth open. Dad even turns his head to look, taking his eyes off the road for a moment. Finally, Mom nods her head.

"That would be nice. That would be *really* nice." She says.

"I'll have to check my calendar," Dad says automatically.

"Maybe it would be relaxing to take some time away from work once in a while," I suggest. "Have some family time that isn't happening because of a jail sentence."

"You don't really have much of a work-life balance anymore," Mom agrees.

Dad chews his lip as he mulls it over. "You're right," he says. "Absolutely right. I need to get some life back. Let's make it happen."

"I'd like that," I tell him. And I mean it. And as long as we are having this strange family bonding moment, I decide to ask. Ever since Devon mentioned his parents, I've had a question in my mind.

"Um, I was wondering . . . where did you guys meet? I know it was college, but what's the story? You never told me."

"Didn't we?" Mom scrunches up her nose. "I guess we skip that one, since it's not exactly a romantic story."

Dad barks a laugh. "You won my heart that night," he says. She smacks his arm lightly in response. "Stop."

I lean forward into the gap between the two front seats. "Okay, now I have to know."

"We were at a dive bar in Philly," Dad begins the story. "It was karaoke night, and I won."

I stare at him as though I've never seen him before. I mean, I knew he liked to sing—I have memories of him singing to me at bedtime when I was a kid.

Wow. I forgot about that.

He still sings along with the radio anytime we're in the car together. He's got a good voice, though I'd never tell him that.

"He was singing Bon Jovi," Mom says, trailing her fingers through the hair at the nape of my father's neck. "What girl could resist?"

"Actually," I interrupt. "It kind of does sound romantic."

"After I was done singing, I saw her from across the room," Dad goes on. "Her eyes locked with mine, and she made her way through the crowd. When she got right in front of me, I was so nervous, it was all I could do to ask her name." He gives a dramatic sigh. "And that's when she threw up on me."

Mom puts her hand over her face. "I'd had a few too many," she admits.

"And you hooked up after that?" I say, raising my eyebrows.

"No, I ran out of the bar," Mom replies. "I was so embarrassed. But I went back the next week for karaoke night, anyway. And he was there. So I bought him a drink to apologize. Seven years later, we were reading *Everyone Poops* to a couple of toddlers."

"How's that for romance?" Dad asks.

I smile and lean back in my seat, turning my eyes to the road and the passing scenery. I actually like that story. That's a story that should be passed down. A snapshot of my parents before they got bogged down by jobs, and bills, and kids, and life.

I have a vision of myself someday telling a kid, *well sweetie, I was on this playground in the middle of winter, and I punched a slide...*

There's a dull ache in the center of my chest, and the warm feeling I had turns to a cold emptiness, the same emptiness that hollowed me out the entire ride up here.

I know I shouldn't have said what I said. But we didn't actually break up.

Did we?

It doesn't feel like we officially did, but maybe that's just my heart wishing it away. Wishing my words away.

This isn't like Devon.

He's always been the patient one. The thoughtful one. The respectful one. He wouldn't just leave things like this. Even if it was over—

Please don't let it be over.

Even if it was over, he'd show me the respect of officially saying so. He just would. I know him.

But you don't, my traitorous mind reminds me. I lean my head against the window, blinking hard to keep the tears at bay.

Devon, where are you?

Can you come over? Now?

DEVON'S TEXT COMES out of nowhere an hour after we get home. After the way we left things—and three days of silence—I wasn't even sure he would ever speak to me again. We're probably broken up. That thought makes my chest hurt and then slides down lower, into my gut.

Do you think he has a gun? Jules's words dance through my head, and I shove them aside. No. I'm not going to think that. Something is wrong, and he needs me. I'm not going to focus on anything but that until I get the rest of the story.

I let Mom know I'm going out and jump in the car. He may live in the neighborhood, but I don't want to give up the extra ten minutes it would take me to walk there. He needs me. And he said *now.*

I park in front of his house and run to the door, my heart pounding. What if I find him broken? Bleeding? Torn apart on the inside but not showing me any physical wounds? What if his parents are there—shouting or threatening? What if he meets me at the door with a bag in his hands, needing a safe place to go? How will I explain that to my parents?

Enough. I've got to stop second-guessing this. I ring the doorbell.

The door opens almost immediately and a wave of relief washes over me at the sight of him looking mostly normal—except for his eyes. They look bloodshot and he has dark circles under them. There's a wariness in them as he meets my gaze.

"Hi." He says.

"Hi." I answer. "I'm here."

He opens the door for me and I step inside.

"I wasn't sure you'd come," he says.

I am your girlfriend, after all, I want to tell him. But I'm not sure of that at the moment. Oh shit. Did he want me to come over because he wants to break up with me face-to-face?

"You needed me," I finally make myself reply.

He sucks in a breath. "Yeah. Yeah, I do." He shuts the door behind me. And I take a moment to look around. From what I can tell, we are the only ones here. The house is quiet.

"So . . . this is what your house looks like on the inside."

"Really exciting, I know," he says, and he tries to force a smile. It doesn't work.

I want to reach out, take his hand, put my arms around him. But I stand frozen, unsure.

"Devon, what's wrong? Is this about our fight? Listen, I'm sorry. Jules ate your dinner. And I shouldn't have—"

He reaches out, putting his hands on my shoulders. "It's not about that. That was a stupid fight. We both said some dumb things. Me, especially. *I'm* sorry."

My breath comes out in a whoosh of relief and I step into him, sliding my arms around his waist and holding him.

"Me, too. I was so stupid. I missed you so much."

He holds me tightly, buries his face in my neck. We stand that way for a long time. Finally, he pulls back and looks at me.

"Can I give you a tour of the house?"

"I thought I came here to talk?"

His mouth tightens into a thin line. "We'll do that, too. After."

He threads his fingers through mine and pulls me through the entry hallway toward the back of the house.

The family room is large and comfortable, with a gas log fireplace on one wall, and a comfy sectional couch across from it. A host of pictures cover the wall over the couch, so many of Devon, at all ages.

"Welcome to the family gallery," he says gesturing at the wall with his hand.

I feel a short twang of jealousy for all the family pictures. Lots of outings in all sorts of places. This is clearly a family that loves to spend time together.

My eyes wander across the photos and then my brow furrows as I realize what I'm seeing. Devon. Lots of Devon. And pictures of Devon side-by-side with . . . Devon?

"That's my brother, Dylan," he says softly.

"You have a twin brother?" I turn and look at him.

"Identical." He smiles, but it's not warm and sunny. The pain in his eyes pulls all the warm out of it.

"Oh, God. You *had* a twin brother."

"He's still alive," Devon answers me. "For now. But he's not doing so good."

I suck in a breath as the realization hits me. *Somebody had better be dead*, I'd said to him the last time I saw him. These past months play back and I study them with new eyes.

"That's who Maya saw at the E.R.," I say.

He nods, pulling me down to sit on the couch next to him.

"We moved here from Florida because Children's Hospital in Philadelphia is the best place in the country for treating injuries like Dylan's."

"That's why he's not in school—he's in the hospital?"

"He was in a care facility that they coordinate with a few miles from here—but he developed complications after his last surgery—they did that the week I was out. They put him in intensive care. He's been battling ever since."

Devon pulls in a breath before he rubs his palms across his knees. Then he pushes to his feet, pacing slowly as he begins his story.

"A little over a year ago, there was an accident. It was stupid. One of those dumb-ass things that happen. We were hanging out at a local park with a bunch of other kids. There was a girl there that Dylan was trying to impress. She had a *really* annoying laugh, but he liked her."

He smiles slightly at the memory and then he shakes his head as if to clear it and goes on.

"We all got this hilarious idea that we were going to pretend we were in The Hunger Games, choosing allies, and throwing sticks at each other like they were spears. We were all laughing. Dylan climbed up a tree to do his best Katniss Everdeen impression. I was on the ground, pretending to die a horrible, prolonged death from genetically-altered mosquitoes. We're talking Oscar-caliber performance. Then I heard the thud."

His hands ball into fists, and his voice carries a note of agony that brings the sting of tears to my eyes.

"At first, we all thought he was faking," he says, as if he still can't believe it. "Dylan wasn't that high up when he fell. He was laying on the ground, and his whole body was shaking. I ran over to him, planning to kick him or something, just for trying to outdo my death performance. But he didn't stop. He just kept on shaking. He was having a seizure. A Post-Traumatic seizure, they called it—it's a sign of traumatic brain injury. He didn't fall that far, but the angle—the way he landed . . ."

"Oh, Devon." I reach for his hand and draw him down to the couch beside me. I wish I knew what to say.

"He's never really come back," he says in a soft voice. "His eyes will open sometimes for a few minutes, but Dylan's not in there. Not anymore. My parents have tried everything. Every therapy. Every treatment—even the surgery that brought us here. They put thalmic sensors in his brain, but it didn't work. It's—it's hard for my mom and dad. They can't just give up. They want so much for this to be fixed. Every expression on his face, every time his finger twitches, they read something into it. I know my brother. Dylan's not there anymore."

I glance over at the fireplace mantle to a picture of Devon and Dylan on the beach, side-by-side with surfboards, tanned and smiling in the summer sun. I can't tell which is which. Their faces—and their happiness captured in that moment—are identical.

"And now he's dying," Devon goes on. "He's really dying. It looked like he might be improving, but he took a turn. His organs are failing. He had a stroke on Valentine's Day, so that's what happened there. I thought I was prepared. I thought I was ready for this. But I'm not, I'm not . . ."

He leans forward and buries his face in his hands. I put my arm around his shoulders and he turns, grabbing me hard as sobs shake his body. My own tears fall onto his neck as I hold him tight, sharing his anguish, wishing I could wipe it all away.

There is no making this better. There is no hiding this wound anymore.

We hold each other for a very long time, until Devon at last pulls away, wiping at his eyes and nose with the hem of his tee shirt.

"Sorry."

"Don't be."

"Sorry for all the snot," he says thickly.

"It's okay. You needed to let it out." I push his unruly hair out of his eyes. "I'm your girlfriend, remember? That's what I'm here for."

"Pretty sure you didn't sign up for excessive snot."

My thumbs gently wipe the remaining tears off his cheeks. "I signed up for you," I tell him. "Snot and all. Secret twin brother and all."

"I should have told you sooner." His eyes drop down, and he's ashamed. I nudge his chin up so that he's looking at me again.

"You had me so worried. I didn't know what was going on—first with the hand being bandaged and that bruise on your head—"

He looks surprised. "I punched a wall," he confesses. "I was having a rough couple of days, after I started school. All I could think about was how much Dylan would have loved Audubon. And Pennsylvania."

"Better than Florida? Better than the beach?"

"The beach isn't that far away here, and he always wanted to learn how to ski."

"I can ski. We have a cabin up in the Poconos, up at Camelback ski resort. I'll take you sometime."

"I'd like that."

I reach up and push his hair off his face. "What about the bruise on your head?"

He looks embarrassed. "The cat really did try to kill me. You thought I was being abused or something?"

"Yeah, I kind of did. Maya saw you—saw *Dylan*—at the hospital in the emergency room. And you would never let me come over and meet your parents."

He nods. "I guess it does seem suspicious. I was just afraid that you knowing all of that would change things between us. Make you look at me differently." He sighs. "And after a while, it got awkward—you not knowing. I didn't know how to bring up the subject without sounding like an idiot or an asshole. I knew I should have told you, but then I'd have to explain why I'm such a head case for not telling you sooner."

"I don't think that. I would never think that. I just wish you felt like you could trust me."

"I do!" He blurts out. His hand comes up to cup my chin. "I do. It's just—you get to a point where you really don't want to talk about it anymore—the situation. I had a year of talking about it and nothing makes a difference."

"This can't be easy to talk about."

"No, it's not. People look at you differently. Or worse, they start telling you about every miracle cure on the internet."

"I know what it's like to have people treat you differently over something that isn't your fault," I remind him. Emotion flickers across his face and my hands slide to his shoulders, giving him a gentle shake. "This wasn't your fault. You know that, right?"

His mouth tightens. "Logically, I know that. But that doesn't stop my brain from going back and remembering that scenario a thousand different ways. If I had just told him not to climb the tree. If I had been paying attention to him while he was up there instead of lying there, trying to get a laugh out of everybody. If I had caught him before he hit the ground. So many 'ifs' but none of them make a difference now. They're just here to haunt me."

"Oh, Devon." His eyes close as I lean up and kiss his forehead.

"I felt guilty for a long time," he confesses. "I still do. It could have been me. It *should* have been me. I had a good therapist—she helped a lot. It was just one of those shitty things that happen to people, and it happened to Dylan. And me. I can't spend my life reliving all that, living in the past. Life doesn't come with a guarantee, Dylan taught me that. I've only got right now, and I'm going to live right now hard enough for both of us."

"We've only got right now," I agree softly. "And right now, you've got me."

Now he kisses my forehead. "Dylan was always the brave one," he tells me. "The tree climber. The adventurer. He was always looking to top himself. At the beach he was the one running hard into the waves no matter how cold the water was. He was the first one to try a new jump on his skateboard. I was always the one hanging back, watching him, cracking jokes and trying to get people to like me because I wasn't as exciting as he was."

"I don't believe that. And anyway, you don't have to be," I assure him. "You and Dylan are different people. Closer than most, because you're twins, but still different people."

The pain he's going through cuts me like a knife. Losing a brother is hard enough. Losing a brother who's been your best friend—your other half for as long as you can remember? Devastating. My mind drifts to Jack. His accident could've easily gone the other way, and I could've lost my brother that night. The thought punches into my chest and my eyes well up again as they meet Devon's gaze.

"I'm so, so sorry, Devon. What can I do? What do you need?"

"Just hang with me for a little while," he says, squeezing my hand. "My dad is on his way back to pick me up. I came home to get a shower, and Dad had to grab some stuff from his office, so I won't be here long. The nurses say Dylan is in process—his body is shutting down. We don't know how long it's going to be, but probably sometime tonight. Mom's staying with him until we both get there so we can all be … so he won't be alone when it's time."

I lean in, kiss his cheek. "I'm here for as long as you need me. And whenever you get back, I'll be here again. All you have to do is let me know."

He settles back on the couch, pulling me in and tucking me into his side. I can hear his heart beating as I lay my head on his chest.

"Tell me about him," I ask, as his finger plays with my hair. "Tell me every little thing you feel like sharing."

"He would have loved you," Devon said. "You probably would've dated him over me. Dylan had a way with the ladies."

"I still would've chosen you."

He gives me a squeeze. "I don't know where to begin," he says.

"You had to have pranked each other," I suggest. "Tell me about some of the ways you used to torture each other." My mouth twists into a smile as I remember some of the ways Jack and I got each other.

Devon lets out a soft laugh as he remembers. "Oh, our pranks were epic. *Epic.* There was this one time, I think we were seven—maybe eight. Dylan laid awake until like, two in the morning, waited for me to fall asleep, and then he hid in the closet. He started scratching on the door. I woke up and I'm whispering at him, trying to get him to wake up, too. I didn't realize I was talking to a pile of pillows under his covers. The next thing I know, he steps out of the closet, wrapped in a blanket like it's a death cloak, and he throws an entire bowl of homemade slime onto my face. I screamed like a goat in a woodchipper. I was sure my face was melting off."

He laughs again, and I laugh with him. It feels good, returning the gift of laughter he's given to me so many times, even if it's at a time as sad as this.

"Epic," I agree. "Tell me another one."

He squeezes me again and kisses my forehead. And for the next half-hour, I get to know Dylan, just a little bit.

THE TONE OF the house is somber. People mill about, sampling from the food spread out across the dining room table, talking in hushed tones. There are flowers everywhere. Devon's parents are stationed in matching armchairs in the front sitting room, facing the door. I meet them briefly, and their eyes light up when Devon introduces me as his girlfriend. They are warm and friendly and it's clear they have questions, but now is not the time.

The funeral was small, just a memorial service. There will be no grave. Dylan will be cremated, with his ashes scattered at sea somewhere off the coast of his favorite beach in Florida.

Devon stands silently beside me, a plate of food in his hand, untouched, just like mine is.

"He'd hate this," he says under his breath.

"What?" I ask.

He gestures with his free hand at all of the people standing around. "This. People making small talk, all sad and everything. I wish I could crank up one of his Spotify lists and start a food fight. That would be more his style."

A smile tugs at my lips. "I'm guessing that would be frowned upon."

"Which is exactly why he'd like it," Devon says. "It would be like giving Death a stiff middle finger. Like he didn't win but he didn't give a shit, either."

Something niggles at my brain and my mind goes back to one of our first conversations.

"That's the villain in your story," I say. "Death."

He nods, then sets down his plate on a nearby end table. "Come on," he says.

"Shouldn't you stay? Your parents—"

"Have got a dozen people in their faces. We're just going up to my room. I need to get away from this for a while."

"Okay." Setting my plate down, he tugs me by the hand up the stairs. I didn't see his room the other day when I was here, and I don't know what I was expecting—colorful posters, maybe some artwork or framed quotes—all optimistic of course. But the room is sparse. No pictures on the walls at all. He notices me noticing.

"I haven't really decorated yet," he says with a shrug. "I've been too busy between school, and the hospital . . ." His voice trails off. "Oh, and I've got a girlfriend, you know."

I step closer and slide my arms around his waist. "I know. I just wish your girlfriend could do more today."

He pulls me in close, and his fingers thread through my hair, stroking.

"You've done plenty. This is all I need. This is life."

And he's right. I feel it. His chest rising and falling, his heart beating, pressed against me. His fingers in my hair make my scalp tingle and the warmth of his body and mine together make a warm cocoon of comfort. In the face of death, in the face of this monstrous loss, there is still life.

He pulls back to look at me.

"I know it's not the best time, exactly, but I didn't give you your last Valentine's Day present."

218

"There was *more*?"

He grins. "I'm all about more."

"I had a present for you, too," I tell him. "It's a gift card to BurgerMania."

He puts his hand to his mouth, and actually manages to force a sheen of tears to his eyes. "That's the most beautiful gift anyone's ever given me," he whispers.

"Too bad you missed dinner. I'll have to cook it for you again sometime soon."

"I'll hold you to that," he says. Then he grabs a package off his dresser and hands it to me.

"You want me to open it now?"

He nods, so I tear the paper off. It's a photo frame, but instead of a picture he took, it's a picture he drew.

"I did that in graphic arts," he said. "Kind of a side project, but I think it turned out pretty good."

"It's beautiful."

My fingers trace the figures in the picture. It's a perfect snapshot of the moment we met, complete with the playground, and me sitting on the bottom of the slide. I'm cradling my sore hand and looking up at him. Devon stands with hands in his pockets, and a beanie on his head, gazing down at me, a slight smile curving his lips.

"The sun is shining," I say, pointing up at the sun shimmering at the top of the picture. "Or is that supposed to be the moon?"

"No, it's the sun."

"But it was nighttime," I remind him. "And it was winter, not summer."

My finger moves down, tracing the green grass and flowers he drew around all of the playground equipment on the ground.

"I remember. But I also remember how I felt when I saw you. This is what I felt. And it was the first time I'd felt anything like that in a really long time."

He pulls me in, and touches his forehead to mine. We stand that way for a moment, just breathing each other in.

"So what now?" I ask hesitantly. "Are your parents going to move back to Florida?"

He straightens up. "They sort of left that up to me. I mean, they both found jobs up here, but they were willing to try and move back if that's where I wanted to be."

"And—?"

"And this is where I want to be." I start to speak and he mashes a finger against my lips. "Before you say anything, I'm not making this decision entirely because of you. You're a factor—a big factor—but I like the idea of a fresh start. Someplace where I don't have to see all the places Dylan used to be. And to tell you the truth, I'm kinda liking the snow."

I feel every kilowatt of the sunshine in that picture now, filling up my insides and shining out of my eyes.

"You want to crank up that playlist?" I ask.

He grins. "On it." He pulls out his phone, finds what he's looking for and sets the phone in a docking station.

He pulls me down on the bed with him and we snuggle into the pillows, facing each other. U2 hums out of the speakers with "I Still Haven't Found What I'm Looking For."

"Dylan was a U2 fan?" I reach up to push his hair out of his eyes.

"He liked them okay. But he loved this song. It's like they cut his veins open and bled him out in the notes and words." His eyes go out of focus, remembering. "Dylan was always so restless. Curious. He wanted to know everything. See it all. *Do* it all. Life was this—this wild ride and he never wanted to get off."

"Like you," I say softly.

He pulls my hand up, twines his fingers with it. "No, not like me. At least, not back then. You know how there's always one outgoing twin and one introvert?"

"Zack and Cody?"

He lets out a chuckle. "If I had a dollar for every time somebody called us that—"

"You could open your own burger buffet," I suggest.

"Goals. But seriously, I know you think I'm super friendly because I latched onto you so easy. But that's not really my first instinct. I had friends, but Dylan *made* friends—and easy. I did stuff, but Dylan did it first. And it was never a contest with him, it's just how we were."

"I wish I had known him." I say, and I mean it.

"You do," he says. "I'm living life for both of us now. I made him a promise while he was lying in that bed that I would wring every single second out of every single day. That I'd make friends, ask the pestering questions, run into the waves, climb the trees—"

"Carefully."

"Carefully," he repeats. "I'm living every day twice as hard. Life can change in a heartbeat, and while you need to have plans, you also need to embrace the unplanned stuff when it comes around. Like a pretty girl punching a slide." He pulls my hand up, kisses my fingers. "Dylan didn't get to live long, but he lived the hell out of every minute that he had."

"Giving Death the middle finger."

"Exactly. So, yeah, Death is the villain in my story. In everybody's story. And you know how you kill Death? You live."

"So lots of skiing, and burgers, and popcorn fights."

"And beach days and picnics and laying on blankets staring at puffy clouds with my girlfriend."

"Mmm," I say, closing my eyes. "I want to do that right now."

"Devon and Blue," he says. "The wind and the sky."

"I love it."

"I love us," he says.

"I love you." The words flow so naturally, and I'm not even a little scared to say them.

His eyes widen slightly, then his whole face lights up.

"Guess that makes me the lucky guy who loves you back."

He pulls me in closer, and his lips touch mine in a slow, searching kiss, not meant to ignite a wildfire, but to affirm the steady burn that makes us both feel alive.

"I like hearing about Dylan," I say, when we break apart. "And I want you to always be able to talk about him with me. Like he's right here in the room. He is, I mean." I reach out and tap him right over his heart. "Right here."

"Hey Dylan!" Devon says rather loudly. "Did I tell you I have a girlfriend?"

He smothers my chuckle with a kiss, but I swear I can hear laughter echoing somewhere, as U2 plays us out.

MRS. LINZA TAKES a seat behind her desk, and I open my presentation. The entire class gives a collective *ohhhh* as the cover of my book appears on the screen. There are even a few laughs.

Mrs. Linza crosses her arms. "I hope you don't think that by choosing a book with less than fifty words, your presentation can be any shorter or less in-depth, Blue."

"That's not what I was thinking at all," I tell her honestly. I turn to the class. "I want to tell you about one of my favorite books, and a book that I feel deserves its place alongside great literature, as something that needs to be preserved for our children, and their children." I gesture to the screen.

"I give you, *Goodnight Moon*."

I get a few more laughs. Mrs. Linza still doesn't look pleased, but she's willing to indulge me, so I go on, pulling up my next slide, which has statistics.

"Published in September of 1947, *Goodnight Moon* is a beloved children's story. It has been reprinted consistently since its release, with an estimate of over fifty million copies sold. It has repeatedly appeared on numerous top one hundred lists for children's stories, and has been translated into over a dozen languages.

This story has resonated with children for three-quarters of a century. Fun fact, *Goodnight Moon* was banned from the New York Public Library until 1972, because the Head Children's Librarian hated it."

"Who hates *Goodnight Moon*?" Devon asks incredulously.

"I know, right?"

I advance to the next slide, one featuring the first page of the book. "Though the language of the book is simplistic, and the book relies heavily on colorful illustrations, the message behind the words and pictures is what makes it worth preserving. You may argue that it might lose something in a purely spoken format, but I disagree."

The next slide comes up, a picture of a child in bed. "*Goodnight Moon* has evolved from a simple bedtime story to something much more important: a bedtime *ritual*."

Next slide—this one is a picture of monks handwriting a manuscript. "Like all rituals, the symbolic language is what carries it forward, repeated down to descendent after descendent. I'm willing to bet many of you in this room know most or some of the story by heart. There's a reason for that.

"*Goodnight Moon* is a story about all the things that surround you. The young bunny first acknowledges everything in the room—alive or inanimate, as if taking stock of all the things that make up their life. The kittens are playmates. The old woman is a parental figure. The listing of all the inanimate objects in the room give us a good sense that the child is well cared for.

"There's a bowl full of mush, so the child is fed, mittens and socks, so the child is clothed. There is a red balloon, and a little house, so we know the child has toys. There's a comb and brush, so we know the child is groomed. There are pictures on the walls, so we know the family values art and culture. And last, by giving an inventory of everything in the room that we can see, we know there are no monsters here. The child is safe."

I move on to the next slide, one of the illustrations from the book, when the light is turned off in the room and the moon shines in through the window.

"Finally, we say goodnight to everything we've just acknowledged. Goodnight to mittens and kittens, to the mush and the brush, and to the little old woman who's whispering hush."

There is a long *shhh* sound as several of the kids in class say that last line with me.

"See what I mean?" I tell them. "It's iconic. And not just because it's a soothing story that can lull your child to sleep. For the record," I say, turning to Mrs. Linza. "That alone should recommend it for preservation. Future parents will thank me."

Mrs. Linza gives a little chuckle and nods her head in acknowledgment. I go on, advancing to my next slide, a picture of a beautiful night sky, full of stars.

"Most importantly, *Goodnight Moon* is a putting away of the things that make up your life on this day. By acknowledging each thing and saying goodnight to it, we put this day in perspective and look forward to tomorrow.

"We say goodnight to the stars, to the air, to the noises everywhere. We are putting this day to rest, and affirming that tomorrow is brand-new and full of possibilities. No matter how out-of-control your life seems today, you can put everything in order at bedtime, and start fresh on a new day. Rest is important. But so are endings. You can't have a new beginning without one."

My eyes meet Devon's, and we hold there a moment before I go on.

"In conclusion," I say, moving to my final slide, a picture of a mother reading *Goodnight Moon* to her child. "*Goodnight Moon* should be preserved, not just for its iconic place in modern literature, but for the contribution of ritual and symbolism it so richly imparts. Thank you."

Everyone claps, and Devon gives me a giant grin and a thumbs up. Mrs. Linza smiles and applauds with the class, so I think I nailed it.

"There was a reason I was scheduled last," I say to the class. And now, with Mrs. Linza's permission—" She nods. "I'd like to welcome a special guest to the class."

I walk over to the door and open it, and there's an audible gasp when Maya walks in.

We stand at the front of the class together, and Mrs. Linza makes her way to the front to stand with us.

"Blue has asked Maya Rodriguez to join us today," she says to the class, "so the two of them can tell you about a new club that's being formed here at Audubon. Girls?"

She gestures with her hand and then walks to the back to lean against the corner of her desk.

I clear my throat nervously and look at Maya. She gives me a nod. I clear my throat again and speak.

"You all know Maya's story, and mine. You know how it is with us," I say. "Or, how it *was* with us. But you *don't* really know her story, and you don't really know mine. We all pass each other in the hall every day. We post about each other on social media. We talk about each other in the cafeteria, in the bathrooms, and at practice. But there's a lot we don't know about each other. Things we don't always tell."

My eyes stray to Devon and he gives me an encouraging smile. I'm about to go on, but Maya takes over.

"Like she said," Maya points her chin at me. "There's a lot we don't know about each other. And sometimes, you need to talk. Or you need someone to listen. We think it would be great if Audubon had a way to help people with that."

"The new club is called Audubon *Right Now*," I say. "Because when you need help, you need it right now. And it should be available to you. We have a few different ways you can access the help you need.

"First, we have a support group that will meet once a week. For the first half of each session, we'll go over stress and coping techniques, including some fun stuff to help ease the tension. The second half of the session will be students talking to each other. It can be something as simple as venting about a bad day or can be as personal as you want it to be. Everything talked about behind those doors stays behind those doors. If there's even a hint of you sharing something from the group on social media or gossiping about in the halls, you're out of the group and facing disciplinary action."

"The second way lets you reach out to us anonymously," Maya says. "On the school website, under Audubon *Right Now*, you'll find a submission form. You won't need to put in your name. Just tell us you need help in the subject box, and when you hit submit, it will reply with a generated ID number."

"The IT department here at Audubon will create a mailbox with your unique ID at Audubon-Academy-dot-info," I tell them. "You'll receive a follow-up email to your student account with a link to access the alternate mailbox. Once you're set up, a peer counselor will respond to your new email address. No student will ever know who you are, unless you choose to identify yourself. Mrs. Ramsey will be working with all of us, training us to be peer counselors. We're looking for volunteers if any of you are interested."

"It'll look great on a college application," Maya adds. "And if you need more help than we can give, we can refer you to outside sources for professional counseling online or on the phone at no cost to you, thanks to a generous grant from the Alumni Association."

My mom really stepped up to the plate, and used every connection in her arsenal to land that one for me. And it's going to help a lot. Maya gives the club flyers to Mrs. Linza, who starts passing them out.

"When it feels like everything's going wrong," I say, "talking can really make a difference."

Maya looks at me. "It definitely can," she agrees. "And it helps to remember that everybody's got their story. And they're all valid."

I smile at her, and look back out at the class. "If you want to share your story, we're here to listen. And to help."

"Right now," Maya says.

"Right now," I affirm.

"Girls, thank you." Mrs. Linza comes back up to the front. "You've put a lot of work into this, and it shows. I hope you all take a moment today to check out the Audubon *Right Now* page on the school website."

Maya gives the class a wave and I walk her to the door.

"Good job," I whisper.

"You too," she whispers back. "See you at lunch."

Have I mentioned that we're going to eat lunch together today so we can work on some items for our first meeting? If this presentation didn't set the whole school buzzing, that certainly will. They'll all be talking. To tell you the truth, we both think it's funny.

I close the door behind Maya, and sit back down at my desk. When I look over at Devon, the warmth blazing out of his eyes is enough to knock me backwards. I want this class to be over. I want this day to be over. I want to be in a little green room, with mittens and kittens and Devon. I want to be holding him—and more. As if he can read my thoughts, he winks at me.

"Anticipation," he mouths.

And I smile, sinking down in my chair.

IF IS SUCH a big word for two letters. *If* can stall your life, if you let it. You can freeze in place, replaying *if* over and over and wishing for a different outcome. You can twist yourself in knots worrying about *if* before you face it. You can retreat from your life like a bunch of Macedonians facing Sparta all because of two little letters.

Or you can talk. And listen. And reconnect. And decide to forgive yourself for every way you think you failed somebody— or failed yourself.

I was always waiting on *when*.

When school is over, when Maya's gone, when my parents can't tell me what to do anymore, when everybody forgets this bad thing, it'll get better. But life isn't about *when*. Life is about *if*. And *if* can be scary. Sure, sometimes *if* ends up badly, but it's also kind of freeing.

When you realize that—when you let it all go—*if* becomes a beautiful possibility. *If* is the beginning of an adventure, or a new friendship, or maybe a quirky romance.

My name is Blue, like the sky. The endless, open sky.

I love it.

ACKNOWLEDGEMENTS

First, I want to thank Stephanie Anderson of Alt19 Creative (alt19creative.com) for her outstanding cover and interior design. You captured this book—and Blue Mancini—so perfectly.

Next, I'd like to thank my editor, Lina Matthews, for her eagle eyes and sharp grasp of narrative. You really helped me find the voice of this piece, and I am forever grateful for your time.

I'd also like to thank Terezia Barna and Zakiya Larry for their solid advice on marketing and publicity. This has been an endeavor, and I've learned so much.

A great big thank you to all my friends and family who broke into frenzied applause at each book announcement, who buy my books and review my books and talk about my books to others. I adore you.

There isn't a thank you big enough for the doctors, nurses, physical therapists and support staff at the University of Kansas hospital for saving my life and showing me how to cope with a life-altering brain injury. I never would have had a "next book" if not for all of you.

And a final thank you to my children, who unfailingly support me, make me laugh harder than anybody, and occasionally call me on my bullshit. You are the very best of my life, and always will be.

ABOUT THE AUTHOR

L.E. DeLano comes equipped with a "useless" Theatre degree that has opened doors for her in numerous ways. Though mostly raised in New Mexico, she now lives in Pennsylvania with two hilarious kids and two ridiculous cats.

Her debut novel, TRAVELER was selected as a Keystone to Reading Secondary Book Award finalist for school year 2018–19 by the Keystone State Reading Association (KSRA) and voted one of The 20 Most Beautiful Books in the World for 2017 by MTV UK.

Website: LEDeLano.com
Twitter: @LE_DeLano
Instagram: @le_delano
Tumblr: @ledelano
Facebook: AuthorLEDeLano
Goodreads: L.E. DeLano

CPSIA information can be obtained
at www.ICGtesting.com
Printed in the USA
FSHW012258191021
85588FS